Kral saw the bod... He could smell ... stolen of life and death—two smells he had never associated with the cave, as long as he had lived. Swallowing, he went in anyway, finding his way through the familiar passage. In the inner chamber he searched for the Guardian, and for that which the Guardian was sworn to protect. He found neither. The Teeth of the Ice Bear, the most sacred relic of the Bear Clan, was gone!

Murdering everyone, putting his village to the torch—those were terrible things, for which someone would pay. Kral swore that even as he made his way from the cave, into the light of day, into the stink of smoke and slaughter, the incessant drone of flies, the leathery flap of vultures' wings.

But taking the Teeth . . . that was a crime compounding the rest, somehow more horrible because it was clearly not an act of war, just the most base kind of thievery. Someone had the teeth; someone had stolen it.

"That someone will pay," Kral declared aloud. "This I vow!"

Millions of readers have enjoyed Robert E. Howard's stories about Conan. Twelve thousand years ago, after the sinking of Atlantis, there was an age undreamed of when shining kingdoms lay spread across the world. This was an age of magic, wars, and adventure, but above all this was an age of heroes! The Age of Conan series features the tales of other legendary heroes in Hyboria.

AGE OF CONAN
HYBORIAN ADVENTURES

MARAUDERS
Volume I

GHOST OF THE WALL

Jeff Mariotte

ACE BOOKS, NEW YORK

THE BERKLEY PUBLISHING GROUP
Published by the Penguin Group
Penguin Group (USA) Inc.
375 Hudson Street, New York, New York 10014, USA

Penguin Group (Canada), 90 Eglinton Avenue East, Suite 700, Toronto, Ontario M4P 2Y3, Canada
(a division of Pearson Penguin Canada Inc.)
Penguin Books Ltd., 80 Strand, London WC2R 0RL, England
Penguin Group Ireland, 25 St. Stephen's Green, Dublin 2, Ireland (a division of Penguin Books Ltd.)
Penguin Group (Australia), 250 Camberwell Road, Camberwell, Victoria 3124, Australia
(a division of Pearson Australia Group Pty. Ltd.)
Penguin Books India Pvt. Ltd., 11 Community Centre, Panchsheel Park, New Delhi—110 017, India
Penguin Group (NZ), Cnr. Airborne and Rosedale Roads, Albany, Auckland 1310, New Zealand
(a division of Pearson New Zealand Ltd.)
Penguin Books (South Africa) (Pty.) Ltd., 24 Sturdee Avenue, Rosebank, Johannesburg 2196,
South Africa

Penguin Books Ltd., Registered Offices: 80 Strand, London WC2R 0RL, England

This is a work of fiction. Names, characters, places, and incidents either are the product of the author's
imagination or are used fictitiously, and any resemblance to actual persons, living or dead, business es-
tablishments, events, or locales is entirely coincidental. The publisher does not have any control over
and does not assume any responsibility for author or third-party websites or their content.

GHOST OF THE WALL

An Ace Book / published by arrangement with Conan Properties International, LLC.

PRINTING HISTORY
Ace mass market edition / February 2006

ISBN: 0-441-01379-1

ACE
Ace Books are published by The Berkley Publishing Group,
a division of Penguin Group (USA) Inc.,
375 Hudson Street, New York, New York 10014.
ACE and the "A" design are trademarks belonging to Penguin Group (USA) Inc.

PRINTED IN THE UNITED STATES OF AMERICA

10 9 8 7 6 5 4 3 2 1

This one is dedicated to all those literary sorcerers—
most notably Robert E. Howard—
who have given so much of themselves
for this reader's joy.

Acknowledgments

This book came about through the efforts of many people, and I'm indebted to all of them. Jeff Conner, who I've known, liked, and respected for decades, and Theodore Bergquist and Fredrik Malmberg at Conan Properties. Ginjer Buchanan, one of the best editors in the business. My old fencing partners, archery partners, and my parents, who moved me to a faraway city where I could touch, every day, a wall built by ancient hands. And, of course, Cindy, Maryelizabeth, Holly, and David.

PACHENIA

MYRKANIA

KHITAI

VILAYET SEA

TURAN

BRINE OF IRON STATUES

AMBULI

KOSALA

VENDHYA

MISTY ISLES

ISLES OF PEARL

SOUTHERN SEA

1

OUTSIDE, THE MOON shone on desert sands, and a chill wind scoured buildings constructed of massive stone blocks. One of these was a giant square structure, the two exposed stories of which gave no hint of the five floors underneath. Deep inside, on its lowest level, Shehkmi al Nasir worked feverishly. The Stygian mage had not tasted fresh air in a week, had not slept or eaten in days.

Nor would he. Too much was happening, too many events that would upend his world were in the offing. He scryed for signs and portents and found more than he could begin to interpret. In a distant desert landscape, torrential rains fell, creating rivers where none had existed before. On a glacier-covered mountaintop, shore birds were seen building a nest. Blood ran like tears from the eyes of a dozen marble statues in an abandoned jungle city. In faraway Khitai, a child was heard crying inside a temple where no children had ever been allowed. And more, and more, and more.

Shehkmi al Nasir tugged at his long, black beard and wondered what it all meant. A connection had to exist between these disparate events, a thread of some kind that could be traced. But he couldn't find its end. All he knew so far was that something was going to happen. Something big. Lives would be lost, others irredeemably changed. Powerful magics would be loosed upon the world.

Any time these kinds of things were in the offing, a powerful sorcerer like Shehkmi al Nasir stood to benefit. He just had to be aware, alert for the opportunities when they arose.

He would be.

He didn't know what form these events would take. But they were coming soon, and he was determined that they would not pass him by. The wisdom to be gained by exploiting them was too great.

Wisdom, and power. And if there was anything that Shehkmi al Nasir craved . . .

KRAL WAS RUNNING for his life when he first saw the girl.

According to the Bear Clan elders, death waited across the Black River. Kral had long made a habit of listening carefully to his elders, then doing what he wanted to anyway.

And it was a good thing he did.

Going too near the fort, which the settlers called Koronaka, could indeed be dangerous. But if he hadn't ignored all the warnings, he would never have spotted the girl with hair of a golden sheen rivaling the late-afternoon sun, with skin as clean and white as the clouds. She was like no one he'd ever seen outside of a dream. So different from the Pictish girls he knew, with their dark hair, arms and legs knotted with muscle, tattooed, painted, or both, and wearing pelts of rabbit or beaver or wolf instead of whatever divine beast had provided its skins for her garb.

He was curious about the fort, though, and the people

who lived there. One afternoon that curiosity got the best of him, and he went to see the fort for himself. Before the truce between them and his Bear Clan, Pict warriors had raided it often, returning, if they returned at all, with souvenirs: weapons, heads, new scars they wore as badges of honor. He had been too young to accompany them.

But since the time of the truce, his people mostly stayed on their side of the Black River and the Aquilonians on theirs. They still told stories of clifflike log walls atop which soldiers marched, wearing so much metal and leather on their bodies it was a wonder they could stand at all. And everyone, the stories claimed, lived together within those walls. Soldiers, farmers, women, children; more people, all told, than in the entire Bear Clan. There seemed to be a limitless supply of them, so many that people wondered if Aquilonia herself were deserted, because all her people were here on the border trying to remake the forests to their own desires. It wasn't that he didn't trust the stories, but Kral needed to see all this with his own eyes.

The Bear Clan lived on a plateau. Not only were the huts of his people reasonably spaced, but where the hillsides sloped away, one could see forest spreading out below for hundreds of miles in every direction. Living within giant walls, packed in like tadpoles in a hand-sized pond, seemed so confining, he was surprised the Aquilonians could even breathe. They were not like Picts, he decided, to whom confinement was worse than death.

So Kral moved silently, stealthily through the forest until he was within sight of the incredible structure. He whistled softly, in spite of himself. It was just as they had said. The fort's people had cut down the tallest trees around to make walls in which to imprison themselves. The fort was bigger than he'd expected; during the time he spent walking around it, examining its features and regarding such of its inhabitants as he could see from outside, the sun moved several notches across the sky.

Even so, it was still just midafternoon when he had seen all there was to see. Walls of enormous timbers, gates guarded from above by bowmen standing on towers. More towers at each corner, also occupied by guards who, while alert, had no idea they were being observed. Other soldiers, who seemed to be a dozen or more feet tall, but who he guessed were standing or walking on some sort of platform built just below the top of the walls. Smoke drifted up from dozens of unseen fires, gathering in a haze that lay over the fort like a blanket, scenting the air with its acrid tang.

Beyond the walls themselves, crops grew in cultivated fields, where even more trees had been felled. The forests were sacred to the Picts, life-sustaining. Kral felt a deep anger growing at people who would so recklessly cut down trees in order to build their odd structures and grow their crops. Men and women worked these fields, accompanied by guards who had grown careless during the years of truce. Didn't they know the forest would provide for them if they only knew how to use it?

Kral believed that if he wanted, he could have taken a head or two from here. But not only would that violate the truce to which his clan's elders had agreed, he had not painted himself for battle or ever killed anyone except in the heat of war.

His curiosity wasn't satisfied. If anything, it was piqued, and he desperately wanted to see what the world inside those great walls was like. Not today, though. He needed to get back across the river, and still try to do some hunting before dark. Reluctantly, he turned away from the fort and started home.

As he did, he saw a strange motion in one of the tended fields, not far away. Looking more closely, he realized it was a bit of whatever skins these people wore. Sometimes Aquilonian traders brought clothing of their kind, to trade for Pictish metals and furs, but the Picts didn't see the value in such things and tended to hold out for weapons or other, more useful, items. So Kral had never held such a thing in his hands. It didn't look like the skin of any animal he had ever seen. He stepped closer, picked it up from where it had snagged on a plant's stem. It was light blue, and felt almost impossibly soft. He turned it over in his hands.

Which was when he was finally spotted, by one of the more vigilant tower guards. "Pict!" he heard a man's voice shout. He knew the word—Aquilonian missionaries had taught most Bear Clan children the fundamentals of their language, years before. And when he glanced up at the tower, he saw the man pointing his way.

Tucking the fabric into his girdle and clutching his spear tightly, he tore into the nearest trees, heedless of thorns and branches scratching and clawing at him. His chest and limbs were bare, with only a belted loincloth covering him, and he was accustomed to the minor wounds that accompanied a run through the woods. As the winter came on, he would wear heavier skins and cover his feet, but that was still months away.

Behind him, he heard the unmistakable sounds of pursuit. A grinding noise that must have been the gates being opened, and the shouts and thunder of men on the heels of their prey. He had a good start, but he was on the far side of the fort, and to get back to the Black River he would have to go around it.

First, however, he struck due south, away from the fort and the river. The Aquilonians crashed through the brush and trees behind, always letting Kral know with their sounds how far back they were. He figured they wouldn't have given chase if they hadn't seen him holding that little piece of cloth. For all they knew, he had torn it off one of their women. Still, he didn't think they'd keep it up for long. He was beginning to feel safe when he broke through some low-hanging pines and found himself facing a rocky cliff, two dozen feet high.

Had he been herded this way? he wondered. No matter—
there wasn't a Pict alive who couldn't scale it. He jumped
up, caught a narrow handhold, started clambering up the
sheer wall. His spear was an impediment to the climb, but
not something he would toss aside.

It was from there, up on the cliff, glancing toward the
Black River, that he thought he saw a girl with impossibly
golden hair passing between a couple of faraway trees. He
craned his head for a better look.

But in slowing to see her, he had exposed himself to his
pursuers, despite the distance he had put between them. An
arrow whistled through the air and bounced off the rocks
not three feet from him. A second thudded into the exposed
root of a tree at the cliff's edge. The archers had the range,
and nearly the aim. Hearing a third arrow streaking right
toward him, Kral simply let go of the cliff face and fell fifteen feet to the ground. The arrow drove into the dirt, right
where he had been clinging.

His fall had cost him valuable time, he knew. Noisy in
the brush, the Aquilonians made steady progress just the
same. And he still had to go around the cliff's base until he
found another way out, rather than expose himself again.

The girl—if she was real, and not a hallucinatory vision
of some kind—was between him and the river to the east.
So he turned west, away from her and his own village,
deeper into Aquilonian territory. He ran along the wall's
base, noting that its top gradually lowered, and the ground
he ran on rose slightly. Soon enough they would meet, or
close to it.

He was right. A short distance ahead, there were only a
few feet of elevation difference. Kral leapt that with a deer-
like bound and reversed direction, heading east now, toward where the wall was taller. As he gained in elevation,
the trees changed. He ran on until he saw one that looked
like it would do. A stout trunk, thick, spreading branches
above, dense with foliage. Behind, the shouts of his pursuers

had settled into the huffing and puffing of men approaching the limits of how far they could maintain their pace through rugged terrain. Kral wrapped his arms and legs around the trunk of the tree and shot up it, ignoring the scraping of his flesh against its rough bark. By the time the Aquilonians reached the tree, he was safely ensconced in its upper branches, peering down between broad leaves at them.

They continued on, not even looking up. Soon enough, Kral judged, they would give up the chase, realizing they had lost him. In the end, it didn't even take as long as he had expected; some of them had already arrived at that conclusion, and they had barely all passed beneath him when they stopped, conversed, and turned back for the fort.

Kral waited another fifteen minutes, by his reckoning, before dropping down from the tree and going to the top of the cliff. He was willing to risk exposing himself here in order to steal another glimpse of the yellow-haired girl he had seen. Even if he was spotted, he believed the settlers had lost their enthusiasm for the chase. The girl was no longer in sight, but he mentally fixed the location where she had been and scrambled down the cliff.

Soon, threading his way through the closely spaced trees, making no more noise than the faintest whisper of wind, Kral approached what looked like a grassy meadow hemmed in on three sides by a wall of thick firs. Where the firs gave way it was to spreading oaks, extending their long, leafy branches. The girl sat in the center of the meadow, on the trunk of a lightning-felled tree that canted toward the ground. Her passage into the clearing, through the grass that lay underneath the oaks, was as clear as if she had marked it with stones.

After noticing her lack of woodcraft, which was always the first thing Kral measured when encountering a new person, the next thing he saw was her hair. He had never seen anyone with hair like hers. His clan worked gold from time to time, but this girl's hair was as if someone had spun that metal, finer than the most delicate thread, then piled it on her head, sweeping it away from her face and holding it back with a wooden device Kral didn't recognize. When she turned her head the sun caught her hair, bathing her in its glow as if recognizing a kindred soul.

Kral wondered for a moment if she was perhaps a goddess instead of a human being. Her skin was pale and unblemished, her arms and legs smooth and rounded like none he had ever seen. She had the same features as everyone else he had ever known: two eyes, a nose, a mouth, ears on the sides of her head; but they were put together in a fashion the likes of which he had never imagined. Her eyes were the blue of the clearest sky, her lips the richest red, her features precisely formed as if by a craftsman's hand. Underneath a pale, nearly white shift of some remarkably smooth material were the curves and bulges of a youthful body growing into full maturity. Threads of gold, accented by her hair and the late-afternoon sun that slanted through the firs toward her, were woven into the bodice of the tunic, which was cinched by a belt of brown leather from which depended a silly, useless dagger. The shift ended midway down her thighs. Her ankles were encircled by the straps of sandals, and on her wrists were golden bracelets.

When he had absorbed her beauty for a few minutes, it occurred to Kral that the girl was entirely unprepared for survival in the woods. Never mind that she was clearly too far from the fort for safety from his own kind, should one of them other than himself happen upon her. The forest held bears, wolves, and other dangers against which she had no protection except that dagger.

But then again, maybe she was divine. The natural and supernatural worlds mingled easily in Kral's mind and the minds of all the Picts. The rising sun and the twinkling stars gave evidence of the activities of the gods, as did the continued supply of beasts in the forests and fish in the rivers, despite the best efforts of the Aquilonians to kill them all. There was nothing to say that this girl was not the emissary of a god or even a goddess herself, in which case she would have little need for steel or other protection against man or beast.

In the end, it was her lack of awareness of his own presence that convinced him of her humanity. A goddess would have seen him, sensed him, even though he kept himself hidden. The girl did not. Despite the evidence of his own eyes, he had to believe that she was flesh and blood,

He didn't want to take his eyes off her, but the sun kept sinking. She would be going back to the fort soon. And if he had any hope of bringing down a rabbit or something else for dinner, he had to be on his way. With one last, longing glance at the most splendid female he had ever seen, Kral melted back into the forest and started home.

ALANYA OF TARANTIA, daughter of Invictus, glanced at the position of the sun. She knew that she should return to the protective walls of Koronaka. She loved being out by herself, though—out where her little brother, Donial, couldn't pester her. Away from the fort, where soldiers and settlers alike seemed to think that a girl of passing beauty was like some art object; to be gazed upon and commented on as if she had no feelings of her own. The men of the fort were not the civilized ones of Tarantia, who could see women of far more stunning aspect on any given day, and they seemed to take Alanya's presence in their midst as an invitation to ogle and leer.

And perhaps it was her own overactive imagination, but some of the women of Koronaka seemed to hold Alanya responsible for the effect her appearance had on their men. She went with them when they left the log walls to pick berries, or down to the Black River to launder their garments, but she never felt part of them. There always seemed to be whispered conversations that excluded her.

So the moments she liked best were those where she was able to steal away by herself. She came often to this meadow, where she could lie in the soft grass or sit on the trunk of the old, downed tree, and daydream. She thought about her girlfriends back in Tarantia, who would even now be preparing for balls or parties to mark the beginning of autumn. Often, she imagined herself back there—back *home*—whenever her father's mission here in the Westermarck was finished. Her time away would give her an aura of the exotic. Boys she had grown up with, who had become men over the intervening span of time, would hardly recognize her because of her own blossoming here in the wilderness. This place was only a temporary stop for her. Tarantia was where she belonged.

Some told her that she shouldn't go off by herself, shouldn't risk being found away from the fort by the savages who had inhabited the woods before civilized man came to settle. Stories were told about attacks by Pictish headhunters in the forests. But the peace between the Picts and the settlers of Koronaka had held for three years, her father said. King Conan himself had sent Invictus here to learn what made this peace so secure, and to travel to other border areas to try to extend it there. Given that, Alanya felt relatively safe in the woods. The stories gave her a little thrill of the forbidden, but nothing else. No savage who hoped to maintain the truce against a vastly superior force would dare lay hands upon the daughter of the king's ambassador.

Today, she watched the birds winging overhead or lighting on the thickly draped green branches to scold and cackle at her. A black squirrel provided entertainment for a time, scampering up and down the trunks as if in search of precious treasure. After a while, she lost herself in memories of home, the trees and grasses of the border region disappearing in favor of the cobbled roads and walled residences of Tarantia. Before she knew it, the sun had sunk low in the sky. Donial would be beside himself with worry, and if she weren't lucky, he would rouse the concerns of others. She might find herself watched more carefully by those in the employ of her uncle, Lupinius, or others.

So without even a last look around at her favorite meadow, which she knew by heart already, she struck out for home, beneath the spreading oaks, then south and west, into the setting sun.

2

"YOUR BROTHER TELLS me that you disappeared to-day."

Alanya fixed a wide smile, even though it felt as if she might break her face. "My brother should tend to his own affairs."

"Nonetheless, he was worried about you."

"I was out with the other ladies, Uncle, picking berries and nuts."

"I see," her uncle said, rubbing a hand across his slick black hair. There was, Alanya supposed, a vague family resemblance between Lupinius and her father, Invictus. Both men had dark hair and eyes almost as black, both had powerful builds with broad shoulders and hands that seemed as big as cooking pots. In spite of his youth—he had seen only fourteen winters, one fewer than she—Donial looked as if he would follow in the same mold.

Not Alanya. She took after their mother, whose hair was every bit as flaxen as her own, with eyes of blue and skin of alabaster. Illness had taken her away years ago, when Alanya was not yet ten, but the girl remembered her mother's aspect as clearly as if her death had been a week ago.

"And what did you do with those nuts and berries?" her uncle asked. "I saw none in the kitchen."

Alanya hesitated for only a moment. "I . . . I gave them to a little girl," she lied. "The daughter of Sharian, who had been unable to gather many of her own."

"I see." Lupinius did not look convinced. He had summoned Alanya and Donial into the dining area of his expansive log-walled home, where they stayed while their father was away on his ambassadorial mission. Alanya would have words for Donial later. Her brother should have known better than to go to Lupinius with any kind of problem. He was their uncle, but neither of them quite trusted him, and Alanya especially wanted his influence over their lives kept to the barest minimum. "I should not have to remind you, Alanya, that these forests are thick with wild beasts, and possibly worse. A Pict was seen just today, very near the fort. We have a tenuous truce with these savages, but they can't be trusted to keep it."

"I know, Uncle," Alanya said. He was right, she didn't need reminding. She just liked to do what she liked to do, and she felt safe enough doing it. Besides, even if she were captured and used as a human sacrifice, as the tales of the old people claimed the Picts did, what worry was it of his? He was not her parent, nor did he seem to want to be. He just liked to control anyone he could. "I was careful."

"Well, see that you remain so," he urged. He turned away, and Alanya knew at once that she and Donial had been dismissed. She restrained the urge to shrug. Instead, she just walked from the room, toward the empty bedroom that had been assigned her when their father had left town. Donial followed. Once they were well clear of Lupinius, she spun around to catch him smirking behind her.

"Why did you complain to him?" she demanded angrily. "What were you thinking?"

The smirk faded from his face, replaced by a sullen, defiant glare. "I do not think you should go off by yourself."

"And I said that I did not!"

"I saw the group of women and girls returning with their baskets," Donial explained. "You came back much later."

"Anyway, why is it your concern what I do?" Alanya demanded. "I am older than you—old enough to be mistress of Father's house, without our having to stay here with Uncle, if only Father could see it." Since their mother's death, their father had been overprotective, treating them as if they had not grown up at all since he had been widowed. Alanya felt smothered by it, which was part of why she liked to get away from Koronaka by herself.

"It is my business, because I am your brother," Donial countered. "And because Father told us to watch after one another. That's all I was doing."

Alanya could barely keep from screaming. *Brothers*. Maybe older brothers were all right, but little ones were nothing but an annoyance.

"Then watch after me, if you will!" she said. "But do not bring *him* into it. And learn when to mind your own business!"

Instead of going to her room, she turned on her heel and headed out the door, into the small town contained by the fort at Koronaka. It was dark out now, but fires and torches lit the town's center, providing plenty of illumination for her to walk around.

Lupinius's house was one of the grandest villas in the town, with its own central courtyard flanked by wings that contained the various bedrooms, kitchen, dining room, storage spaces, and other chambers. In the courtyard a great variety of herbs, spices, and flowers grew. Its front gate faced the bulk of the civilian homes in the little town, houses occupied by the families of soldiers as well as the merchants and tradespeople who provided necessary goods and services to them.

Arranged around Lupinius's place were the barracks of his Rangers, a military force loyal to Aquilonia but more specifically, to him. Behind the barracks was an array of official buildings, including the governor's house and his administrative offices. Adjoining this area was a basilica containing public buildings, grain storage, and, ranked along the interior colonnade, a number of shops and taverns. A temple to Mitra stood nearby, with four steps leading up to a small, enclosed building, topped with a peaked roof. Finally, closest to the parapeted log wall that faced out toward the Black River, stood the military barracks, row after row of wood-framed buildings that housed the fort's soldiers. A tower stood at each corner of the wall, so the soldiers could keep watch toward the Thunder River, which flowed at their backs, even though the greatest threat was presumed to come from the Pictish clans across the Black, to the fort's west.

A man came around the corner, headed in her direction. A soldier, by the look of him. Moments later they both passed beneath one of the torches that lit the boulevards at night, and recognized each other. It was Calvert, one of Lupinius's Rangers. He was a hard-looking man, with narrow slits for eyes, a thin-lipped sneer of a mouth, and a thick, muscled build. He wore a belted tunic, leather breeches, buckskin boots. A short stabbing sword hung at his side. "Good evening, Alanya," he said. "What brings you out so late?"

"Just walking," she replied, with a smile. "I am allowed to do that, am I not?"

"Of course," Calvert said. She suspected that humor was completely beyond his capabilities. "But it can be dangerous at night—I would hate for you to get into any trouble."

Alanya looked around. Sometimes there were—as at home in Tarantia—brawls that spilled out of the taverns, occasional thievery or murder, or drunkards just out for a good time who picked the wrong people to harass. But that night, the town was as quiet as a cemetery.

"No trouble," she said simply.

Calvert nodded as if she had imparted some great wisdom. "All right, then," he said at last. "Good evening to you."

She watched him wander off, and wondered if he'd just come from a tavern himself. When he was out of sight, she continued her own aimless roaming, into the more populous area of the basilica.

Townspeople and soldiers alike nodded to Alanya or greeted her by name as she walked. Her father was well-known; therefore, so was she. In almost every way, she preferred Tarantia, a city of sufficient size that she could be anonymous. In the fort, any misbehavior at all would be noted by a score of people who knew her father or uncle. Not that Alanya hoped to misbehave—she just wanted to be able to if she chose.

So she didn't. Instead, she just walked through the town, enjoying the crispness of the early-autumn air, the sweet scent of night-blooming flowers, and the freedom from the oppressive presence of her uncle.

IN SPITE OF her brother's meddling and her uncle's warnings, two afternoons later Alanya was back in her clearing. The day was warm, with only a few clouds scudding across the blue sky. That warmth put her in a dreamy state of mind. She lay on her back in the thick grass, watching the breeze vibrate the needles of the towering pines and the birds wheeling about overhead, their wings catching sunlight and throwing it down toward her like darts. A girl needed some time alone, she had decided.

Time to think, time to plan for the future, time to wonder and dream.

She had seen no sign of the dangerous wild animals her uncle had warned her of, no sign either of Pictish warriors on the march. She felt every bit as safe here as she did in Koronaka, and far more at ease because there was no one staring at her, no soldier or merchant wondering when she might be willing to take a husband.

She guessed that she had been in the clearing less than an hour when a shadow detached itself from the trees and walked toward her. Her heart hammered in her throat at his appearance. Her hands quaked uncontrollably. If she had been standing, she doubted her knees would have supported her weight.

As he passed from darkness into light, she saw what he was—her uncle's worst fear, become horrible flesh. A Pict, she was convinced. Probably only a year or two older than she was. His shoulders were wide, his chest broad and flat. A brief loincloth draped around his waist provided his only coverage. His dark brown hair was pulled away from his face and kept back by an unseen band, but a wide copper one encircled his wrist, and a narrow band of copper, joined with leather, hung at his throat. A wicked-looking knife hung from his girdle.

But he also carried a spear, and he made a point of laying it to one side before he approached her. His face was surprisingly handsome for a savage, with a strong jaw, clear dark eyes, and high cheekbones. His mouth was set in a smile that seemed at once tentative, yet genuine. She didn't know if that meant he was looking forward to beheading her, or perhaps grilling her flesh for his dinner, or whatever it was Picts did to their captives according to the stories she had heard.

If he had in mind taking her prisoner, though, wouldn't he have kept the spear? Not that he'd need it to stop her if she tried to run or fight—the muscles of his arms and legs

bulged with strength. Still, the action had the feel of something done to reassure her that he meant her no harm.
Whether he did or not, the next few moments would tell.
He was already too near for her to hope to escape. Alanya
forced herself shakily to her feet and tried to greet him
with a friendly grin.

He stopped a few feet away from her and stood with his
arms hanging loosely at his sides. His brow knitted as if he
was concentrating deeply, and he spoke.

"Hello," he said, in ragged-accented Aquilonian. "I
am . . . Kral."

"Kral?" Alanya echoed, astonished that he spoke instead of simply attacking. And her native tongue, at that.
"I'm Alanya. You speak Aquilonian?"

A cloud seemed to pass over his face, and she guessed
that he was busy translating her reply. Finally, he answered her. "A little," he said. His accent was so awful
that she had a hard time understanding the words. But
he spoke slowly and uncertainly, which helped a bit. "A
missionary . . ."

She understood immediately. She had heard of a few
missionaries who had gone into the Pictish wilderness in
search of souls to save. Some were immediately sacrificed
to whatever dark gods the Picts worshiped, others returned
horrified at what they saw there. But a few had stayed for
years, teaching the savages the tongues and ways of civilized society. Likely this young Pict had encountered one
of them and learned some of the Aquilonian language.

"Of course," she answered. "You learned it from a missionary."

Again the brow knitted, almost comically. "Yes."

Perhaps the missionary had also trained him not to eat
human flesh. She could hope, anyway. "I am from Aquilonia," she told him. "My name is Alanya, daughter of Invictus of Tarantia. I'm staying at Koronaka, with my uncle,

and . . ." She let the sentence trail off, realizing that she was going much too fast, no doubt confusing him.

"I am sorry," she said. "I will try to speak more slowly."

He shook his head, looking completely lost. "Slow," he repeated.

Alanya put her hands together and drew them apart leisurely. "Slooow," she said as she did so.

He duplicated her motions and her phrasing, speaking the word at the same languid pace that she had. "Sloooow."

"Right," she said. She had begun to relax now. If he were a threat, he would have already made some move toward her, rather than engaging in verbal play.

She tried to point in the general direction of Koronaka. "I live there," she said. "Koronaka."

He pointed toward the west and spoke a word that she couldn't make out. She guessed it was the Pictish name for his home, but it just sounded like a guttural growl to her.

"Why are you here?" she asked him. "Across the river from your home?"

He touched his own face with his first two fingers, just under his eyes, then drew them away again. "I come," he elaborated, "to look at you."

3

KRAL BECAME ALANYA'S little secret.

She would go to bed playing over in her head the talks they had, and wake up anticipating their next meeting. The days seemed to drag interminably until she got a chance to escape Donial and Lupinius, to escape Koronaka and get to her clearing in the woods. Kral seemed to enjoy their time together as much as she did—rarely did she arrive that he didn't show up a few moments later, emerging from the shadowed trees like some sort of phantom.

His Aquilonian had turned out to be very basic indeed, but he was intelligent, a quick study, and Alanya found it easy to teach him new words, even for difficult concepts. Before long they were engaging in wide-ranging conversations. Kral seemed amazed and impressed by her stories of life in Tarantia, though he could scarcely believe that so many people could live in the same "village." And Alanya listened in wonderment to his stories of barbarous life—hunting; battling against settlers or, more often, other Pictish clans; skinning animals with his bare hands, teeth, and knife, boiling their brains to tan their hides. His love of the forest was contagious, and he knew a variety of special places: fast-flowing creeks and grassy glades and trees of unimaginable beauty. Alanya had never thought there was much here except empty space where she could find refuge, but Kral convinced her that there was beauty in the forest on its own terms, that the trees, grasses, and animals had charms that were unlike anything Tarantia had to offer.

She enjoyed keeping him a secret, someone whose company she enjoyed but about whom she would say nothing to another living soul. At the same time, there was a loneliness to it. She often found herself wanting to share the strange and wonderful stories he told. She decided to save them in her memory. When she was safely back home, she could regale her friends with them. Here, the settlers would just want Kral captured or killed. When that realization set in, she knew she could never truly be at home among such small-minded people.

Back in Koronaka, Lupinius confessed that he was worried about her. She had taken to long periods of silence—periods during which she was perfectly happy, thinking about some tale or other that Kral had told her, or remembering some bit of woodcraft he had taught. Lupinius assumed these were mournful or sad moments. Of course, she couldn't tell him that he was completely mistaken. Despite the fact that Kral had never put a hand on her except to help her across a rushing creek or to dust the grass from the back of her shift, Lupinius would be horrified at the idea that she had any contact with one of the savage Picts.

Alanya, frankly, couldn't even picture Kral cooking and eating her, or any other human. He did mention human sacrifices and severed heads in some of his stories, which was horrific enough, but he gave no indication that she might become the subject of one of those barbaric religious rites. Nor did he treat her as someone he might want to enslave, or even take back to his clan as a wife. He seemed content to talk, to explore the forest and show her what he knew of nature, and to enjoy her company, just as she did his.

When her father had told her that they would be living on the border of the civilized world for some indefinite period of time, she had been virtually heartbroken at the thought of leaving her friends, her home, the only life she had ever known. Actually arriving at Koronaka after the overland journey had done little to dispel that sorrow. Getting to know her uncle Lupinius had only made things worse.

Now, finally, she had found something precious here on the frontier, something that was hers and hers alone, and which made her happy to rise every morning. It was an idyllic time, and she found herself wishing it would never end.

FOR HIS PART, Kral was happy to keep Alanya's presence concealed from the rest of the Bear Clan. They lived in a truce with the settlers of Koronaka, and did some trade with them. But there were those within the clan who would insist that Kral had no business associating with one of them, especially a young woman. They would demand that he either kill her or bring her to the village. It was time, some said, for Kral to think about taking a wife and building a family of his own. If he was really so taken with her golden hair and delicate face, then she might as well be the one.

To be sure, such thoughts had crossed his mind anyway. But he truly valued her spirit, her willingness to teach and be taught in return, and her enthusiasm whenever she saw him. If he took her captive, he was afraid she would lose that. Better by far simply to be her friend, to meet by secret in the forest and spend time with her that way. If at some point things changed, then they could discuss her joining him in the Bear Clan's village.

On this particular day, he came to her with a heavy heart. Every young man of the Bear Clan had to go away by himself for a time on what the Picts called a Spirit Trek, to live naked and alone in the wilderness, to seek inside himself for the spirit that would accompany him for the rest of his days. These journeys had no fixed end point, concluding only when each man had discovered his spirit. Some were gone for days, others for months. Kral had to leave, though, and he had to tell Alanya that it would be some time before he would see her. If her father decided to return to Tarantia while he was away, then they would never be together again. The realization was almost too awful to bear, but there was nothing to be done about it. It was simply the way things were.

Before he even had a chance to tell her, she pulled something from beneath a cream-colored gown that was more elaborate and formal than most that she wore out here. She had taught him the name of the material, which was silk, and explained that it was woven by insects. He had a hard time envisioning that, but was willing to take her word for it. It was even softer than the fabric he had found in the field—softer by far than anything traded by the Aquilonians for Pictish copper or furs.

The object she held out before him was round as the full moon, only with a handle about as long as the spread of his fingers was wide. "Look at this, Kral," she said excitedly. "It belonged to my mother. The last memento I have of her. I always keep it beside my bed."

She handed the thing to him. He held it gingerly, looking it over. There were gems encrusted in the surface of the main disk, blazing red and green and blue in the day's bright sun. The handle was barely as thick as two fingers, shaped like two intertwined worms joining at the bottom. Kral had not a clue what it might be used for, but the workmanship was impressive.

"Nice," he said.

Alanya laughed, a sound he always equated with cool water trickling over rocks. Her golden hair was pulled back and tied with ribbons of red and yellow. He thought once again how lovely she was. "Turn it over, silly," she said.

He did so, and in his shock he dashed the thing to the ground. His right hand dropped to the hilt of his knife as he stared at it. But then he looked at Alanya, and her expression was startled, crestfallen—not the look of someone who was playing a joke or trying to trap him in some way.

"It's just a mirror," she said. She squatted down and picked it up, then held it toward him again.

The side that was not bejeweled was perfectly smooth, like a pond on a windless day. As in such a pond, he could see his own reflection. He had seen himself in water and polished steel enough times to know what he was looking at. But as he allowed Alanya to draw closer with it, he realized he had never before seen himself with such precise clarity. The scar that bisected his left eyebrow, courtesy of a bobcat he had wrestled with eight springs before, was plainly visible. So was the longer scar that ran up the line of his jaw, on the right, from a fight he'd had with a couple of members of the Raven Clan two summers ago. He smiled, remembering that their scars at the end of it had been worse than his. And as he did, even his smile was reflected in the object Alanya held. A mirror, she had called it.

"Is it . . . something magical?" he asked at length.

Alanya giggled again. "My father has hinted that it might be," she replied. "For myself, I have never seen it do anything except show reflections, and there's nothing magic about that."

Would his fingers pass through the surface, or ripple it like water? Almost afraid of what might happen, Kral reached out to the mirror's face and touched it. His fingers left streaks on it, but that was all.

"I should like to be this mirror," he said, "if you look into it every day."

Alanya's fair skin went crimson, and he knew he had spoken too rashly. Before she could reply, he filled the silence. "I must leave," he said. "On a . . . a journey."

The red glow faded from Alanya's cheeks. "But you'll be back soon?"

"I know not," he told her. He wanted to tell her that he would try, that he would make any promise he could, but the Aquilonian words wouldn't come to him. Even the Pictish tongue seemed to fail him, or his own mind did. He didn't know what he wanted to say, much less how to say it. Instead of speaking, he took a copper band from his wrist, handed it to her. "A . . . memento," he managed, echoing the word she had used earlier to describe the mirror.

Alanya was very pale now, her lower lip quivering. She thought for a moment, then reached down and ripped a narrow strip of cloth from her gown. Silk, he reminded himself.

"A memento," she said as she handed him the silk. He held it in his hands for a moment. It was almost weightless, and as smooth as water, or the surface of the mirror. Then he wrapped it around his forehead, tied it in place. She slipped his wristband around her upper arm, where it held snugly in place.

He wanted to say more, or to take her in his arms, or something. But the Aquilonian tongue had utterly abandoned him, and at any rate he had never learned the words for a situation like this. Anyway, he had to be going. There would be feasting tonight, in honor of his quest, and he couldn't be late. In the morning, before first light, he would be on his way. As it was, he had tarried too long.

"Good-bye, Alanya," he said, remembering the words for that, at least.

"Good-bye, Kral." She held his gaze for a moment, but then turned away from him. Feeling discharged, he picked his spear up off the ground and started into the trees, bound for home.

• • •

ALANYA HAD WANTED to keep looking into Kral's eyes, wanted him to elaborate further on what he had said about wanting to be her mirror, a statement with a certain fierce barbaric charm that even the smoothest boys of Tarantia couldn't match. But tears had filled her eyes unexpectedly at the thought of his leaving. She had to look away. When she blinked them clear, he was already becoming one with the shadows.

She was torn between sorrow and rage. Why had he said something like that now, today of all days? Why had he not made his feelings clear earlier, when he wasn't going away? And why did he have to go, for that matter? Where? For how long?

The clearing in the woods had no answers for her. Before, it had seemed like a little circle of paradise on earth, but now it was just a bare spot where the trees wouldn't grow, where lightning had blasted the one brave enough to try it.

Now that she knew Kral wouldn't be here, she doubted that she'd be coming back either. She had practically worn a trail through the grass, beneath the oaks, all the way from Koronaka. She would follow that trail back, but that would be the last time she would use it.

She was almost to the trees when she saw Donial, half-hidden behind the trunk of one of the oaks, staring at her with wide, fearful eyes.

4

"YOU ARE SPYING on me!" Alanya charged as she stalked through the tall grass toward her younger brother.

Donial's mouth worked for a moment with no sound coming out. He backed away a few steps, until he ran into a low-hanging branch from one of the oaks.

"Ow," he said, stopping suddenly and rubbing the back of his head. His dark hair was thick and wavy. He blinked his big dark eyes at Alanya a couple of times. She had wondered for a couple of years if he would ever grow into his own facial features—his eyes and full, red lips seemed too large for his head. "You were . . . that was a *Pict!*"

"I know that," Alanya said.

"Did he hurt you? You were crying."

"He would never," Alanya insisted, sniffling a little in spite of herself. "He is very nice."

"But . . ." Donial pointed toward the copper band on her arm. "Did he give you that?"

"He is my friend," Alanya said. "Not all Picts have to be brutish savages, you know."

"That's not what Uncle says."

"Uncle, in case you hadn't noticed, is not always right about everything." When they had first arrived from Tarantia they had been allies in their distaste for Lupinius. Since then, Donial seemed to have been won over to their uncle's side, more and more. It worried Alanya, made her question her brother's judgment.

"But all the others say it, too. The Rangers—"

"They work for Uncle," she pointed out. "Of course they agree with him.".

"Still—the whole fort, the soldiers . . . everything exists because of the Picts, to keep Aquilonia safe from them. What makes you think they are all wrong?"

Alanya huffed in frustration. "I never said they were," she countered. "Just that not every Pict is evil, any more than every Aquilonian is good."

Donial stared at her as if she had uttered some unspeakable blasphemy. "You are lucky to be alive."

"Donial!" Alanya shouted. "I told you, he's my friend!"

"Where did you meet him, then?"

"Right here, in the clearing."

Donial suddenly twisted his head from side to side, a look of fear crossing his face. "Are there more of them?"

"Do you think they surround us?" Alanya asked, with a laugh. "How many ways do I have to say it? He would not hurt me. He would not surround me. He has never been anything but kind and perfectly proper."

Donial nodded, more to himself than to her, as if he had just reached a difficult decision. "I'm going to tell Uncle."

"You cannot, Donial," Alanya said. She was aware that she was close to pleading, but didn't care. "You must not. He won't—"

But Donial wasn't listening. Instead, he had spun around on his heels and started back toward Koronaka at a full run. She half hoped that he would dash headlong into a tree—it would at least slow him down enough that she

could get home first. Maybe she could persuade Lupinius
to ignore the boy's crazy tale . . .

Not trusting the fates, she took off at a run herself. Donial was faster than she, however—he had always been a
good runner, speedy and tireless. She gave chase as well as
she could in her long silk skirts, but he had every advantage. Kral had taught her to move noiselessly through the
forest and how to avoid the low branches and thorns. But
even so, even as clumsy and . . . and *Aquilonian* as he was,
Donial still outpaced her. Before long she could hear him
crashing through the woods ahead, but couldn't even see
him. She slowed, beginning to dread reaching Koronaka
and the miserable reception that would certainly greet her
there.

It turned out to be every bit as bad as she feared.

THE THING DONIAL was best at was speed.

Every boy had some skill or ability. Some were big and
strong, others so tough nothing would hurt them, still others exceedingly smart. Donial was not any of these, he
thought—he was small, wiry, and didn't much care for pain
or scholarship.

But he was fast. In footraces, even against men twice his
age, he usually left everyone else choking in his dust. He
had acquired a reputation around Tarantia for it and knew
that there were even those who gambled on his races. Bet-
ting against him carried a certain disadvantage, but he did
lose from time to time, and on those occasions the payoff
was significant.

So when he ignored his sister's pleas and took off
through the tall grass, he knew there was no chance she
could catch him. Alanya was strong and fit, but she was no
match for him when it came to speed. He heard her voice
behind him, becoming more muffled with every long
stride.

He knew he should have run the moment he saw her with the Pict. But he had been so astonished at the sight, he had been rooted to the spot, watching. If she had needed help, there wouldn't have been much he could do—though he would have tried anything and everything. But the Pict was at least a head taller than him, with a much longer reach. He looked more powerful in every way, and in hand-to-hand combat Donial's quickness might not have made much difference.

So running for help would have made the most sense. The fort was a couple of miles away, but he could have been back with soldiers, or some of Uncle Lupinius's Rangers, in just a few minutes. If he hadn't trusted in his own speed, he'd never have left the fort to begin with, given the stories he'd heard about Pictish savagery.

Fetching soldiers would take too long if the savage had decided to slit her throat, but they'd be quick enough to help if he had wanted to carry her away to his own village.

Instead, he had just stood and watched until the Pict was out of sight. His response didn't say much for his own physical courage, which had never been so tested until that moment. Of course, the young savage hadn't seemed to be physically threatening her. His doing so might have made things different—might have spurred Donial to some more definitive action.

At any rate, as he dodged trees and rocks, he knew that despite Alanya's entreaties, he had to tell Uncle Lupinius what he had seen. Alanya didn't like, or trust, their uncle, a fact she had made abundantly clear since before they even reached Koronaka. Donial had agreed with her, at first, because he knew no better. But the more he got to know the man, the more he liked him.

Invictus, their father, and Lupinius, his brother, had been born to people of accomplishment but no significant wealth. They had managed to acquire some land, a small estate, and had served king and country honorably. Invictus, as the

oldest son, had inherited that estate. He worked hard on be-
half of Aquilonia. But so did Lupinius, who had been left
with only a small sum, no fortune at all, which he had
quickly spent. Without the inheritance, Donial believed
that Lupinius had had the harder time, and he had per-
formed admirably. He was a man of ambition who had
overcome the disadvantage of his birth order to create a
significant estate of his own, albeit in the border region instead of the city. Alanya claimed that their father sent
Lupinius gold from time to time. But Lupinius had never
given any indication that her story was true, never inti-
mated that he had established himself in Koronaka through
anything other than his own efforts.

Since Invictus had gone off on his mission to the other
border outposts, Donial had been spending more and more
time with Lupinius, and the more he did the more he found
that he liked and respected their uncle. Therefore, he didn't
share Alanya's distrust of him, and he thought that
Lupinius, having put in a good many years in the Westermarck, would know what to do about the encounter Donial
had witnessed.

Something had to be done. Alanya was his sister. He had
to take care of her.

Maybe he couldn't kill the savage, but he could use
what skills he did have.

He could run.

Really fast.

"SHE IS MY niece, Governor Sharzen," Lupinius stated
later that day. "That . . . that heartless savage assaulted her.
Honor demands action against him and all his kind."

He was in the governor's office—the only one in Koronaka, he judged, that was bigger and finer than his own.
The interior walls were plastered, the windows shuttered,
the wooden floor covered with rich Ophirean rugs. Sharzen

sat on a pile of luxurious silken cushions beside a low table
of intricately carved pine. On that table rested a cask and
two cups, which Sharzen had filled with good Zingaran
wine when he had entered. Lupinius had left his un-
touched.

"We have a truce," Sharzen replied, as if Lupinius were
a child. He was a big man, a Gunderman, well over two
meters tall with sandy brown hair and blunt features. He
wore a tunic of forest green, with a short cloak fastened to
it by silver pins. On his wrists were coiled bracelets, and a
broad leather girdle belted his thick waist. "It was agreed to
by representatives of King Conan himself. I cannot simply
break it on a whim."

Lupinius fairly exploded. "A *whim*? He laid hands upon
my niece. When Invictus hears, do you have any doubt that
he'll counsel Conan to drive every last one of them into the
sea?"

"But . . . she said that he never touched her. She called
him a friend, Lupinius. He gave her a gift."

"She knows not what she says," Lupinius shot back.
"The poor girl was terrified. It is her brother whose testi-
mony we must believe."

"I suppose there is some truth to that," Sharzen offered.

"You know that it is absolutely true. And here is something else to chew on, Governor. I have my own force of
Rangers. We will go over the river and into the Pict village.
The truce will be considered broken then anyway, whether
our presence there is officially sanctioned or not. But if we
are outmanned, then the savages will have reason to strike
back here, at Koronaka. Possibly the other clans will set
aside their petty squabbling and join together against you.
If we go in with our full forces—my Rangers and your
regulars—then we stand a chance of wiping them all out in
one swoop."

Sharzen looked a little pale, but he drained his cup of wine
and his color returned. "You make a good point, Lupinius."

"Of course I do," Lupinius said, knowing he had the man convinced. Now it was just a matter of establishing the details of the raid and making sure that he was in charge. That wouldn't be too difficult. Sharzen was an appointee of the king, a soldier who had served Aquilonia well in these territories many years ago. He had helped found Koronaka, more than a dozen years earlier. But since trading in the sword for the quill and the trappings of power, Sharzen had become weak. His massive muscles became flabby, and his once-strong will turned toward the bureaucrat's goal of self-preservation at all costs. Any courage he might once have possessed had been buried over the years by a desire to serve his distant masters in order to retain his position.

At Koronaka, Sharzen governed two hundred settlers and as many soldiers. And yet he had ceded his own authority to Lupinius without a fight. Lupinius couldn't help but feel contempt for the man Sharzen had become.

The good thing was that his fears made the governor that much easier to manipulate. Since learning that, Lupinius had been able to use the man's position to build his own fortunes, until he was himself the most influential person at Koronaka.

She didn't know it, but Alanya had given him the means to increase both wealth and power—to make of him someone who could go back to Aquilonia a very rich man, to build a comfortable estate and get away from the stinking border territory forever.

As an important man, rumors and whispers usually found their way to his ears. He had, for months, been tantalized by a story of an incredibly rich Pictish hoard, kept in hiding by the Bear Clan. Traders who went back and forth across the river heard stories from friendly Picts, or ones trying to tempt them into better deals. Gems from caverns deep beneath the hills they ruled, the whispers claimed, nuggets of pure gold that they didn't even know how to

work. Items stolen from travelers or settlers who ventured
too close to Pictish territory. They kept these things because they were shiny and pretty, Lupinius guessed. People
who still dressed in raw skins and painted themselves for
battle had no need of wealth.

But he did. He could put it to much better use than they
ever would.

As long as King Conan's truce held, however, he'd had
no opportunity to go in search of it. If the Picts wouldn't
break the truce, then he would, and Donial's tale of the Pict
he'd seen with Alanya gave him the excuse he needed. Attacking the village with the full force of the Aquilonian
border soldiers and his own Rangers, taking them by surprise, they would be able to slaughter the Bear Clan to a
man. Then he could take his time locating the hoard. Once
he had that, combined with the wealth he had already
amassed in his time on the Westermarck, he would return
to his homeland.

Their father had favored Invictus, and as a result his
older brother had inherited the bulk of the family's land
and prestige. Lupinius had been obliged to make his own
way in the world. He had bitterly resented Invictus for that.
From time to time Invictus had offered Lupinius what
amounted to charity. Each time, Lupinius had accepted the
proffered gold, and each time found himself despising his
brother more than ever. Now, on the cusp of great riches,
he thought that perhaps he could find it in himself to forgive his brother after all.

Either that, or put his newfound wealth to work to
ruin him.

He just had to decide which it would be.

ALANYA WENT TO the cabin that she and Donial shared
with their father when he was at Koronaka. It was not

nearly so grand as Lupinius's home, or as the home she was accustomed to back in Tarantia. But its small rooms and low ceilings were still somehow comforting, compared to the more expansive space with which Lupinius had surrounded himself. The walls were built of rough-hewn logs chinked together with Black River mud, the floors and ceilings of the same wood, split and planed. Lupinius's place had water from the river and a timber-lined sewage system, but at the more modest cabin her father had acquired, they had to use the nearby public latrine.

She needed time alone, though, and this was the best place to get it. Donial had become comfortable at Lupinius's place, and no one else in town ever came to her father's cabin. She could have the solitude she wanted here, time and space to think about what had gone wrong.

Maybe she should have told Donial about Kral from the beginning. Had she enlisted his help in keeping the secret, he might not have been so inclined to run screaming to their uncle when he did find out. But she didn't expect that he'd actually follow her. That seemed like too much effort, even for him.

Instead, finding out the way he had was so shocking, he'd just had to tell someone. And since he had been gradually becoming closer to Lupinius, maybe even seeking their uncle's approval, going to him with the stunning news had seemed like the right thing to do. Perhaps it was. If their places had been reversed, wouldn't she have wanted to reveal what she had seen?

She had thought that Lupinius would be furious. Instead, he acted concerned, even solicitous. The expression on his face when he took her into his office was warm and concerned. "Did he hurt you?" he asked. "Touch you in any way?"

"No, Uncle," she had said. "He was a gentleman."

"That is hard to believe, of a barbarous savage."

"It is true just the same."

"Very well, then. I am glad to hear it. Still, you understand that it was a very foolish and dangerous thing for you to do, correct?"

He had sat down in a straight-backed chair made of branches with leather strapping, leaving her standing before him. He rested his muscular forearms on the chair and stared at her with a dark-eyed gaze that seemed to bore right through her. "I understand that under ordinary circumstances, it would have been," she hedged. "But in this case, Kral would not have allowed any harm to come to me."

A sharp intake of breath, and Lupinius brought his right hand to his chin in exasperated fashion. "I am not sure you fully comprehend the situation," he told her. "There will have to be a response."

She didn't know what he meant. "A response?"

"We cannot allow those Picts to think they can just come across the river at will and consort with our women," he explained. "There are strict rules about contact between our peoples. There will be bloodshed. Brave soldiers might lose their lives, because you were so foolish as to wander away from the fort unescorted and because you didn't immediately report this person's approach."

Alanya was confused and furious. If the bloodshed was a direct result of contact between Pict and Aquilonian, then what would it have mattered if she had told her uncle about it right away? And why did anyone have to suffer, since she had been unhurt and unmolested? Didn't traders deal with the Picts on a regular basis, albeit on their side of the river? And what of her own father, who had been to the Bear Clan village on several occasions?

Lupinius had been unwilling to provide any further detail, claiming a pressing engagement with the governor. He had left the house. Shortly after, so had she. That was when she had come to the cabin, where she sat in the dark, fighting back tears, clenching her fists so tightly that they hurt, wishing there was some way that she could magically undo the whole day and start over again with the dawn.

5

INVICTUS RODE THE borrowed steed hard, trying to cover ground as quickly as possible. The road was a narrow path cut between overhanging trees, which blurred into a wall of solid green. Dirt flew beneath the animal's hooves at every stride.

He had been at Thandara, trying to negotiate a peace between the Pictish Eagle Clan and the settlers there. But a rider who had just spent a few days in Koronaka had mentioned preparations for an assault on the village of the Bear Clan. King Conan had specifically sent Invictus to Koronaka to learn how they had kept the peace and to share that information with other settlements throughout the Westermarck. For that truce to be broken was bad enough. Worse yet was the rumor that Invictus's own brother, Lupinius, was a chief instigator of the impending attack.

So the mad rush back toward Koronaka. Governor Diocletian of Thandara had offered an escort, but Invictus had been afraid that additional companions would only slow him down. Besides, until Lupinius broke the peace Invictus had little to fear from Picts, and he could deal with any bandits who might try to make trouble. He spent one night camped near the road, on a bed of soft needles dropped by towering pine, and breakfasted on dried beef and crusty bread given him by Diocletian. With the first light of dawn he was back in the saddle.

The second afternoon, Koronaka loomed ahead of him, its dark brown walls and towers solid and forbidding. Were he a naked savage living in a mud hut, he thought, he would not want to do battle with people who could build such a structure from the materials surrounding them. He shouted a greeting to the guards at the gate, who threw it open to admit him, and in a flash he had ridden past them into the fort's parade area.

He was dismayed by the sight that met him there. The previously peaceful settlement of Koronaka had turned into a war camp. Smiths worked furiously over fires that spat sparks into the afternoon sky, mending armor, shoeing horses, shaping swords and spears. Fletchers busily produced arrows by the hundreds. Bare-chested men drilled with sword and axe, sweat running in rivers down their torsos in the hot autumn sun. Others, who Invictus judged to be either more dedicated or insane, trained in full armor.

Standing on a shaded porch of the governor's house, watching the bustle of activity, were Lupinius and Governor Sharzen himself. Invictus threaded his horse through the preparations for war and dismounted before the house, tying the animal to a nearby post. Lupinius watched him approach with a welcoming smile on his face; Sharzen's expression was more tentative.

"Welcome, brother," Lupinius said. He was resplendent today in red silks, and his face looked flushed, as if his skin were trying to match his attire. "You're just in time."

Invictus waved an angry hand toward the busy parade ground. "It looks as if I'm a little late," he growled.

"Not at all," Lupinius said. He moved forward and

embraced Invictus awkwardly. "Your daughter is fine, by the way. Unhurt and completely safe."

"Alanya? What does she have to do with anything?" Invictus demanded.

"Surely you got my message," Lupinius said anxiously. "About the Pict boy?"

"I received no message," Invictus replied simply. "If I had not heard that you intend to break the truce, I would be in Thandara yet. What Pict?"

Lupinius drew Invictus to one side, as if to exclude Sharzen from the conversation—though the man had not so much as opened his mouth since Invictus had arrived. "I am sorry, brother," Lupinius said. "I assumed that my runner had reached you there. Alanya was away from the camp, and met a boy in the woods—a young man of the Bear Clan. He did not touch her or threaten her in any way, she insists. Nonetheless, I thought the only appropriate response was to attack the clan's village, to let them know in no uncertain terms that any kind of fraternization between their men and our women will be met with a harsh and definitive response."

A rush of horrific images presented themselves to Invictus's mind's eye. Alanya with a Pict boy? He had made great efforts toward making peace with the Picts, working to convince the leaders of other settlements that while they were different than Aquilonians, they were no less human beings. But that didn't mean that he would trust one alone with his daughter. He had been to a few villages where Aquilonian women had been taken as wives, and while he hadn't seen them mistreated, it was still not a fate he wished for Alanya.

"I need to see her," he said. "Right away."

"She has been keeping to herself the last few days," Lupinius said. "But I know she will be thrilled to see that you've returned."

"And we need to discuss this assault on the Bear Clan,"

Invictus said. "I am not convinced it is necessary or wise."

Now Sharzen decided to add his input. "The decision has been made," he stated. "We cross the Black River at first light."

"But . . . she is *my* daughter," Invictus said, surprised at the governor's adamant response. "I should have some say as to how we respond."

"You were gone," Sharzen said. He looked pale, as if arguing with Invictus was a frightening proposition for him. He was a big man, but Invictus knew that his physical strength was much greater than his personal courage. He blinked rapidly as he spoke, and his gaze rested somewhere over Invictus's shoulder instead of directly on him. "Lupinius spoke for you. And I made the final decision, as governor of this territory."

"I am here now," Invictus pointed out. "And able to speak for myself. And for the king, who desires peace along the border."

"The king is not here, and does not know what has transpired. At any rate, we are too far along to stop. The appetite for battle has been whetted. If we tried to halt the action now, our soldiers would fall upon one another. There is considerable emotion stirred against the Bear Clan as a result of this, and some of the soldiers would doubtless make for their village anyway."

"As would my Rangers," Lupinius added confidently.

"A smaller force might well be rebuffed," Sharzen continued. "Certainly you would agree that a defeat for us would be worse for the peace than a resounding victory."

"And no battle at all would be even better for the peace."

"No battle is no longer an option," Lupinius put in. "There is only a win or a loss, now. I prefer to win."

Invictus remembered his brother as a young boy, fiercely competitive at every game they played. "As you always have," he said.

"So you are with us?"

"I have not said that," Invictus countered. "I need to see Alanya and Donial."

"You will find them at my house," Lupinius assured him. "Safe and well."

Invictus bit back his frustration at his brother and the governor, knowing it would do no good to unleash it on them. "Very well," he said. "I trust that nothing will be done until I have spoken with you again."

"First light," Sharzen reminded him. "With or without you."

Invictus stalked away, trying to ignore the man's comment. Sharzen's boldness no doubt had to do with Lupinius's presence and the fact that he was on his own home ground. Invictus knew that, one-on-one, he could persuade the governor to his own views on nearly any subject. But he had fallen under Lupinius's sway, and for some reason Lupinius was determined to attack the Pictish village. Invictus wished he could know his brother's mind. What was he after, across the river?

He had heard from time to time that the Bear Clan guarded a great prize. Nothing an Aquilonian would find valuable, he was sure. The things the Picts cared about were meaningless to civilized people. He had assumed it was something of religious significance to their dark gods, but of no import to anyone else.

Was that it? Could Lupinius have heard such stories and become determined to find whatever it was the Bear Clan kept?

Alanya was simply an excuse, he knew. A justification for something Lupinius wanted to do.

Something that would have more far-reaching consequences than Lupinius had imagined, he was sure.

Breaking the peace here would be a blow to King Conan's border pacification efforts, and to his own prestige in the king's eyes. But the hot yellow disk of the afternoon sun already lowered toward the western horizon. He had

precious little time left to come up with a way to preserve
it. From the sound of things, a visit to the Bear Clan village
would not help, either. Even if he persuaded them that danger loomed and they should hide, they wouldn't stay away
from their homes forever. Once the soldiers crossed the
river, the truce would be over.

Lupinius's house wasn't far away, and Invictus was
there in a few minutes. The clanging of steel on steel
echoed through the lanes as he walked, mirroring the conflict he felt in his heart. His duty to his country was to
broker peace, but if his duty to his family contradicted
that . . .

He banged through the front door and called to his children. His shout was answered immediately by two voices,
and Donial and Alanya both rushed into the room and
threw their arms around him. He held his children, breathing in their scents, relishing their presence. Though Donial
more closely resembled him and his brother Lupinius, both
reminded Invictus of Marta, his wife, and he was eternally
grateful that she had left him these gifts before the sickness
snatched her from him.

After catching up with them and describing briefly how
he had been occupied during his absence, he sent Donial
away and took Alanya into Lupinius's study. They both sat
down, and he looked her over carefully. She seemed sad,
her eyes red and puffy from crying, but otherwise she was
the same girl he had left just weeks before.

"Tell me about this Pictish boy," he said.

Alanya looked as if she might begin to weep again. "I
cannot believe that Governor Sharzen is sending soldiers
to punish his village," she began. "He did not even do anything wrong. We only talked."

"But how did you meet him? Why were you alone, away
from Koronaka?"

"Life is so boring here, Father," she said with a sniffle.
"You cannot imagine what it's like, especially when you're

gone. I just had to get away from everyone, to be by myself for a time."

Invictus remembered feeling the same way himself on occasion, during his own youth, though it had been passed in and around Tarantia. He supposed it was common to people of Alanya's age. Still, not a good enough reason to put oneself in danger. "You can't just leave the fort on your own, Alanya. It isn't safe out there."

"I felt perfectly safe," she insisted. "Kral would not have hurt me. I have said the same to Uncle Lupinius, and Governor Sharzen, and anyone else who would listen. He needed someone to talk to, the same as I did. We were friends, nothing more."

"An Aquilonian girl cannot be friends with a Pictish boy," Invictus stated flatly.

The skin of Alanya's pretty face was turning red, almost edging toward purple, as she answered. Tears began to flow from her eyes. "But I was. Everyone says there's something wrong with it, or with me, but Kral and I were just talking and learning about each other's lives. What could possibly be wrong with that? Is that not what peace means?"

Invictus sighed. "You are idealistic, Alanya. There is nothing wrong with that. It's the province of youth. But now things have been set in motion that I do not think can be changed. You can be as idealistic as you want; but you also have to understand that your actions have consequences, and they're not always the ones you would have preferred had you been able to choose."

She sniffed again and looked at Invictus through her tears. He wished there was a way he could wipe away her pain, ease her mind of the anguish he knew she felt. She hadn't intended anything like this to come from her private excursions, and if she truly liked the Pict boy, she wouldn't want anything to happen to him in the coming battle.

It seemed there was nothing anyone could do about that

now. Sharzen and Lupinius had seen to that. The best he could do would be to go along, to try to keep the carnage to a minimum and do what he could to restore the peace after their little adventure was over.

It wasn't perfect, but he couldn't see any other options.

6

"OH, DONIAL," ALANYA said later, in her brother's room. "If only you hadn't told Uncle . . ."

"I had to, Alanya," he complained. "I had no choice."

"There is always a choice!" she shot back. He sat on his bed, and she leaned against the closed wooden door. He had already changed into clean white nightclothes, but she remained fully dressed. "You could have just believed me when I said that we were friends and that he would never hurt me."

"He is a Pict," Donial pointed out needlessly. "And not to be trusted."

"Obviously, it is you who is not to be trusted," she said. "The first hint of a secret, and you go running to tell."

"Alanya, you know better than that." He looked genuinely hurt—which had, after all, been her intent. He had caused her plenty of pain the last few days. He had fallen under Lupinius's sway, that much was clear. "You can trust me."

"It would be nice if I could," she said. "You are my only brother, after all. I would rather be able to trust you than not, but so far you have not demonstrated that I can."

"What do I need to do?" he wondered. "What can I do?"

"I know not," Alanya replied. "I suppose the next time you have a chance to keep a secret, you should keep it. Otherwise, I will wonder if you really want to be a brother to me at all."

She knew she was being harsher on him than he might have deserved. But outside, soldiers were preparing to march in defense of her honor—honor that had not been threatened in the first place—because of Donial's report to Lupinius. There was nothing she could do to stop it, now, and the helplessness she felt caused her to strike out at the nearest available target.

Which was Donial, her unfortunate brother.

His bad luck, she thought. She tossed him a shrug and opened the door, letting herself out. She would get precious little sleep tonight, she knew. Let him see if he could claim any for himself.

DRESSING BY TORCHLIGHT, Calvert donned a green wool tunic that came just short of his knees, then strapped on a leather cuirass, slipping a shirt of mail over the top of that. The interlocked metal rings jingled softly as he fastened greaves by their metal straps to his legs, then strapped on arm guards. Buckskin boots followed. Finally, a belt from which he could hang his dagger and sword, and a helmet with cheekpieces, a neckguard sticking out in back, and a browguard in front. All this equipment was stored in the front room of the barracks in which he lived, one of several arrayed around Lupinius's house. Around him other men did the same thing—some grimly silent, like him, others joking and laughing to defray the tension they all felt. The air in the room was close, tinged with sweat and iron.

Sharzen had made clear that Lupinius would be the military commander of this mission, even though the soldiers of Koronaka were nominally under the command of Gestian, an Aquilonian captain. So far from home, normal standards were often not followed, and here Lupinius's Rangers had just as much status as the regular army soldiers did.

That was fine with Calvert. He had joined the Rangers as a mercenary, traveling from Nemedia in search of someone who would pay in gold for the use of his fighting arm, and if necessary, his blood. Lupinius had been willing to part with the gold, so he had joined the man's forces. He had seen some action in Lupinius's employ, and had occasionally been well paid just to sit around protecting his boss from unseen, probably imaginary, enemies. He had worked his way up to the rank of captain, so he would be in charge of the fifty Rangers, relaying Lupinius's orders to the men and translating them into effective tactics.

Calvert glanced over at his friend Rossun, who was shoving his sword into his scabbard and drawing it out again. Rossun was years younger than he was, strong but with little experience in battle. "Not much room in here for that," Calvert said. "Maybe you ought to practice outside."

"Merely checking the slide," Rossun returned. "I need no further practice—just Pictish flesh in front of me to cut."

"Be sure you wipe it after you do," Calvert reminded him. "Last thing you need is putting away your sword bloody and having it stick when you need it next."

"I know," Rossun said. "Happened to a Gunderman I knew once."

"And don't know anymore, I'd wager," Calvert guessed.

Rossun laughed and raised an eyebrow at him. "Right."

A hammering sounded on the outer door of the barracks. Calvert knew what that signified. "Time to move out," he said.

"I am ready," Rossun answered. Other Rangers responded similarly. Fully garbed, they started out the door to join the ones already outside. Everyone knew the Picts were unmatched at woodcraft, and it would be nigh impossible to sneak up on them in daylight. So the plan was to cross the Black by night. The Picts would still know they were coming before they arrived, but not by much. Regardless of what defenses they could manage in that time, the larger Aquilonian force would overrun the small village and destroy it.

Lupinius had made one thing extremely clear—there were to be no survivors.

That, also, was fine with Calvert. He had no love for the Picts, who piled the skulls of their victims around their huts just to enjoy the view. All he loved was the gold that Lupinius paid him. Each month he sent as much as he could home to his wife in Aquilonia, against the eventual day when he would give up the service of others, buy his own land, and they would live out the rest of their days in comfort.

In the meantime, whoever found himself on the wrong end of his sword would suffer for his mistake.

INVICTUS HAD RESIGNED himself to the idea of battle. Lupinius would not be dissuaded, and since he had known Sharzen much longer than Invictus had, there was no getting to the governor, either. So the truce would be broken by midmorning, and there was nothing he could do to stop it. Years of effort by dozens of ambassadors would be for naught. He couldn't help wishing that Lupinius and Sharzen would have to tell King Conan in person what they had accomplished, when the dust cleared. Both would, he believed, be carried away from that royal encounter on their shields.

He had marched toward the Black River alongside the rest of the soldiers. He would try to keep the bloodshed down, to make sure that the soldiers obeyed reasonable rules of warfare. He was afraid his brother was capable of atrocities matching those of the Picts, and felt his relationship with the Bear Clan would enable him to intercede if necessary.

They moved through the forest as quietly as several hundred armored men could move. At the river, they crossed in any way they could—some in skiffs or small boats, some on makeshift bridges, others wading or swimming. Soaking their armor wasn't the best preparation for battle, but it was unavoidable—the Black River was the natural dividing line between their territory and that of the Picts, and to take the time to bring the whole force across on boats and bridges would allow the enemy too much time to prepare defenses or leave the area altogether.

Now the thin light of predawn paled the eastern sky, though here among the trees it remained dark. Invictus had tried a couple of times to talk to Lupinius—not to turn him away from his goal, since it was too late for that, but to try to determine what it was, besides his plainly exaggerated concern for family honor, that he was after in the village of the Bear Clan. He knew his brother too well to trust him fully.

Lupinius wasn't talking, though. He seemed strangely somber, as if the nearer they came to the Pictish village, the more he regretted something.

Or lusted after something. No telling which. Either could have caused quiet reflection in Lupinius.

The landscape changed as they neared the village. The Picts had built their village on a flat table at the top of a rocky slope. Trees thinned and became more stunted as they came closer, and Invictus knew that it had been a strategically sound place to locate their homes—anyone attacking would have to give up cover and attack uphill. At the same time, if the Picts chose retreat over battle, they simply had to slip down the other side of the hill and into more of the deep woods, where their native skills would serve them well. But eventually they would return to this place, which was sacred to them, so that would only be the most temporary of solutions.

Sensing their proximity, the soldiers stopped even their whispered jokes and curses. To a man, they approached their goal silent, grim-faced, serious in the bloody chore that lay ahead. Invictus was glad of that much. They were engaged in dirty work here, but at least they weren't gleeful about it. Only on Lupinius did he think he sometimes saw a self-satisfied smirk, when his brother didn't think anyone was looking.

Trey, one of Lupinius's Rangers, approached him as they neared the village. "They have seen us by now, have they not?" the man asked. He was a Bossonian, and he held his traditional longbow in strong, large-knuckled hands. His brown eyes were barely visible in the half-light.

"Yes," Invictus replied. "Likely as soon as we crossed the river, or shortly after. We've passed by at least a dozen lookouts by now, each one signaling our progress back to the main force."

"And yet they have not attacked us?"

"Their best position is on the hill," Invictus explained. "They cannot hold us off indefinitely from there, but they can make advancing hard on us, and they can send many of us to hell as they go."

"Why not flank them, then?" Trey asked. "Send some of our men around to the other side of their camp and come at them from both sides?"

"You would have to ask your master, Lupinius," Invictus replied. "This is his plan, not mine. But I think the answer lies in expediency. To get around them we would have to have landed another force earlier, and the Picts could have fought them as they tried to get around. Unless we had time to land an army by sea, from the Western Ocean, and allowed them to approach that way, there is no easy way to flank them. A frontal attack, up the hill, without cover, is the best we can do on short notice."

Trey nodded. He had probably figured out the answers for himself, Invictus guessed, but wanted someone else to tell him he was correct. "Nearly there, are we not?" he said.

Invictus pointed ahead, through the scrawny, twisted trees toward a sloping landscape of granite dotted with small clutches of vegetation. The sun floated in the sky behind the hill, making it hard to see who or what was on top, but he could make out dozens of wooden huts with scurrying figures darting about between them. Some of them formed themselves into ranks at the top of the hill. "We *are* there," he agreed.

The soldiers came to a stop, and the sound of their halting was like distant thunder. Invictus knew the Picts were armed and just waiting for them to charge. Even if they had been sound asleep, they were awake now. Might as well have approached with torches and drums. None of the normal forest noises could be heard; no insects or birds sang their usual songs.

As the men stood waiting, Lupinius worked his way through them, toward Invictus. "Here we are, brother," he said when he made it through. "Are you ready to avenge your daughter?"

"She needs no vengeance," Invictus replied angrily. "This is your campaign, brother, not hers. Do not pretend otherwise. Whatever you hope to accomplish here, let it be on your head. And I hope you find it worth the price."

Lupinius shrugged. "We are here now. The whys of it don't matter anymore. Only the killing."

Invictus shook his head. "I wish I knew where you learned your lust for blood," he said. "Not at the knees of our father."

"I wish I knew how you developed your fear of it," Lupinius countered. "So I can make sure it never happens to me."

Invictus had nothing further to say to his younger brother, and apparently Lupinius felt the same way. He turned away from Invictus and drew a short sword from its scabbard. Raising it high, he brought it down fast and banged it against his shield. "Attack!" he shouted, at the top of his lungs. "For Aquilonia!"

"For Aquilonia!" hundreds of voices echoed.

Invictus didn't return the battle cry. He knew that this was not an attack for Aquilonia at all.

But he drew his sword, just the same.

7

TREY AND TWO dozen of his Bossonian fellows, most in the employ of Lupinius's Ranger troop, raised bows toward the sky, nocked arrows, and let them fly at the Pictish ranks. They could have used another half hundred bowmen effectively to pin down the Picts, but made do with what they had available.

As soon as one arrow was airborne he plucked another from his quiver and set it in place, then drew the string to his cheekbone and let go. The air was full of the twanging sound of bowstrings and the rush of arrows, then the clatter as they struck rock or shield, and finally, happily, the occasional scream as one found its target. Beneath the flurry, the Aquilonian troops dashed up the hill, spears out, swords drawn, shields at the ready.

They had barely reached the rocky slope when arrows came their way, as well. The Pictish archers were nestled among big rocks at the top of the slope, or hidden behind their huts, where they couldn't be seen from the base of the hill. They fired volley after volley, just as the Bossonians had. Their shafts were shorter, their points more crudely struck, but their arrows, tipped with poison made from forest plants, rained death just the same.

After the first ten arrows, Trey decided to get more selective in his aim. The Picts were too widely spaced for random volleys to do much damage, so he looked for individual targets. There a naked warrior reached for an arrow of his own, from a quiver slung across his back. Trey sighted down his arrow, then raised its point to compensate for height and distance, and released. The Pict had barely raised his own bow when Trey's arrow plunged into his breast. The Pict dropped his bow and turned, knees buckling beneath him. Trey could see the point of his own arrow jutting from the man's back and blood pouring out the wound, then the man fell to the ground, snapping the shaft.

Trey nocked another and looked for his next target.

CALVERT WAS PART of the first wave up the slope.

Rocks clattered everywhere around them as the Picts fought first with the most common objects at hand. He raised his shield and batted them away, dodging the bigger ones that rolled toward him. Arrows came next. Calvert saw the man next to him die, a feathered shaft vibrating from his ruined forehead.

Loose rocks slid under his booted feet as he climbed. He kept his head down, helmet toward the enemy, shield held up to block any oncoming missiles, and tried to maintain his balance. He had no doubt that the Picts knew full well how hard it was to fight on loose scree, and they probably kept the hillside that way intentionally.

He was determined not to die there, two dozen feet or more from his foes. If he fell this day, it would be in honorable battle. Gritting his teeth, he dug his feet into the dirt and pressed onward.

A few feet ahead of him, one of his Rangers caught an arrow in the gullet and spun backward. A young soldier dodged the falling corpse with a shout of dismay. Calvert swatted the soldier's rear with the flat of his sword. "Get on up that hill, you worthless whelp!" he ordered. "Don't let a few bodies scare you!"

The soldier gave him a hurried nod and redoubled his efforts. Calvert knew their strategy wasn't complex or particularly subtle. It depended purely on the Aquilonians' having sufficient numbers to overwhelm the Picts' defenses. Which meant many would die in the effort.

Nothing could be done about that. Calvert drove himself onward, glancing up just long enough to see a Pictish archer at the top of the hill drawing a bead on him. He zigged to his right and at the same time reached down and scooped up a fist-sized rock. Lurching to his left, then back to the right to confuse the archer's aim, he paused just long enough to hurl the rock toward the man. The archer was still, trying to release his arrow, and he let it fly just as the rock crashed into the bridge of his nose. Blood spurted, and the archer swayed back on his feet, dropping his bow.

With another few long strides, Calvert reached the first rank of Pictish defenders. Arrayed around him were other Aquilonians, both regular army and Rangers. From the grunts and cries, he knew the real battle had begun.

Rough-hewn spearpoints jabbed at him from every direction, and the air was filled with the bellowing war cries of the painted Picts. Blocking some with his shield, others with his sword, he tried to push deeper into the line. He twisted out of the way of one. Another's grazed the outer side of his left thigh, drawing blood. Calvert snarled, batting away another with his shield as he focused his efforts on the Pict who had cut him. The man was short and stocky, bronzed from the sun, his blue-painted skin naked but for a ragged loincloth, some pounded copper rings about his arms, and a necklace of sinew and bone. His lips were drawn back, baring teeth in a savage grimace. Fear blazed like fire in his eyes as Calvert bore down on him.

Calvert ignored the rest of the fighting going on about him and slashed at the Pictish spearman. His blade cut into the staff of the Pict's weapon, and Calvert yanked it back, releasing it. The Pict screamed and jabbed his spear forward again. Calvert swung his shield up into the broken shaft, and the weapon snapped. Calvert pressed his advantage, drawing his sword back for another blow, which the Pict tried to block with only the remaining section of his spear. Calvert's sword bit deep into the man's neck, cutting off the Pict's death cry. Calvert had to press his foot against the dying man's chest and tug his sword to free it from the muscle and bone in which it had lodged, and when it came loose, blood ran its length like a river.

At last, one of the barbarians had fallen under his sword. Calvert blew out a breath he hadn't realized he was holding as a wave of satisfaction swept over him. Looking left and right, he saw that some of his fellows had fallen; but more were advancing, their heavier armor and better weapons carrying them forward through the nearly naked Picts.

Behind the defenders stood their village, rows of small thatched huts made of branches and mud, with fire pits, animal corrals, and public areas interspersed. More Picts streamed from behind the huts, bearing daggers, short swords, and spears. One of them roared to the heavens, holding aloft by the hair the head of an Aquilonian he had decapitated. Calvert wondered if Lupinius had known how many defenders there would be when he had hatched his plan.

But his sword had tasted blood, and would do so again. He let loose with a battle cry and waded into the stream of Picts, sword flashing and flailing, the thrill of battle filling his heart.

•   •   •

INVICTUS'S HEART WASN'T in the battle, but he knew
that his allegiance to his fellow Aquilonians demanded that
he not turn his back on it. He waited behind the Bossonian
archers while the first wave stormed the hilltop village,
then joined the second group as they charged up to rein-
force the first. He noted that Lupinius held back, seemingly
directing the battle even though no one actually fighting
could hear any of his commands over the cries and clatter
of war.

The slippery hillside was spattered with blood and littered with the corpses of the fallen when Invictus climbed,
his long sword clutched tightly in his fist. By the time he
reached the top, the battle had already turned in favor of
the attackers. There were plenty of Picts remaining, and
they fought furiously, caught up in the battle frenzy that
was typical of their kind, but the Aquilonians and their allies were in control of the situation. Invictus spotted a
wounded Pict scrambling to his knees with a bow in his
hands, hoping to bring down a soldier or two before he
died. With a swift kick, Invictus let the Pict know that he
was not alone. The man turned, surprise widening his eyes,
and Invictus drove the point of his sword through the
man's breast.

That foe dispatched, he turned his attentions toward the
village. Carnage filled his senses—the stinks of sweat,
blood, and fire; the roar of flames gutting wooden homes,
the clang of weapons, the shouts of the victorious and the
cries and whimpers of the vanquished. Everywhere, he saw
smoke and bodies and blood, and, through the haze, warriors fighting to the death.

The sight sickened Invictus, but he knew it was the price
of war. Same with the burning of the huts, most likely done
with torches drawn from the Picts' own fire pits. It was not
until he had dispatched a few other stragglers and ventured

farther into the village that he discovered that it was not an isolated atrocity. The bodies of Pictish women and children were strewn about the landscape along with those of their warriors. Rangers loyal to Lupinius carried torches and moved in methodical fashion, setting each hut aflame in its turn. It dawned on Invictus that these were not random acts, carried out in the heat of battle. The Rangers looked like they were following orders, and they were absolutely merciless in their dedication to duty.

Invictus looked about him for his brother. He felt the hand of Lupinius behind this outrage. But Lupinius was still far down the hill—climbing, but not hurriedly. Invictus knew they'd have to have a talk about this atrocity, and he suddenly began to look forward to the exchange.

Until then, however, he'd have to find some way of containing the damage. Breaking the uneasy truce was one thing—slaughtering every man, woman, and child of the clan and putting the torch to their village was something more. When news spread, it would threaten the peace along the entire Pictish-Aquilonian border. If he could salvage anything from all his efforts, he had to act immediately.

He saw a Ranger named Rufio raising an axe toward a young woman with black hair and flashing eyes. She had been running from a hut after it was torched, heading for the back side of the hill, and escape, but the Ranger blocked her way, and his blow looked as if it could cleave her in two. "Hold!" Invictus shouted, his voice deep and commanding.

Rufio barely glanced his way. "Why?" he asked.

"What is she to you?" Invictus demanded.

"I might ask you the same."

The woman had fallen to her knees. She knelt there, looking furious enough to kill, as the two argued over her fate. "A civilian, not a combatant, for one," Invictus said.

"There are no civilians here," the Ranger replied. "Look, she wears a knife in her girdle."

That much was true. Most Picts went about their lives similarly armed. The knife might have been used for cleaning game, cutting meat, or working with skins. Still, Invictus couldn't deny that it might have been used as a weapon, as well.

"She looks as if she'd use it on you, given a chance," Invictus observed.

"She no doubt would," Rufio returned. "I don't intend to give her that chance."

"Let her go," Invictus urged. "If she'll promise not to fight."

The Ranger shrugged. "I have my orders already," he said, confirming what Invictus already suspected. He turned back to the woman, who spat angrily at him.

But only once. The Ranger's arm rose and fell, his axe flashed in the morning sun, then her blood sprayed wetly across the dirt as the life flowed from her.

Invictus turned away in disgust. He had been to the Bear Clan's village on several occasions. The village elder was an old man called Cuirn. He was not the clan's war chief—that was Ondag, a ferocious warrior whose bloodied corpse he had already passed, surrounded by those of several Aquilonian regulars. But Cuirn was respected by all, and his opinions were not taken lightly. His hut was toward the back of the village from here, facing out toward the rising sun on the eastern rim of the hilltop. Lupinius's Rangers were moving from the west side back. Maybe they hadn't yet reached him.

Invictus weaved his way between knots of battling warriors, pausing now and then to add his sword stroke to the effort. Picts were falling by the score. Their blood coated his arms, legs, and armor. But he felt a pressing urgency, so he tried to avoid the clutches of combat and worked on getting his bearings through the smoke and madness of battle. The huts looked so similar to one another that he had to make an extra effort to locate Cuirn's, but finally he saw it.

He started toward it when a young Pictish boy, probably not more than thirteen, charged at him from the open door of a nearby hut, its doorway decorated with human skulls hanging from leather thongs. The boy had a short spear in his fists and a look of rage on his face. For a moment, Invictus wondered if it was that boy who had made friends with Alanya. If not him, then one like him—a friend, perhaps, or kin. Then he put those thoughts out of his mind, because the youth obviously intended to kill him.

He deflected the first thrust with his shield. The boy didn't give up, though. He slipped the spearpoint under the shield's edge and tried again. This time the iron tip scraped across Invictus's mail, and he took an involuntary step back. The spear came toward him once more, but he brought shield and sword together, trapping the shaft between them. Invictus twisted and drew the boy off-balance. Then he shoved forward with the shield, and the boy buckled under his advance. Invictus let the shield hang by its straps and grabbed the spear with his left hand, wrenching it from the youth's hands. Then he hurled it far from the boy, fixed him with a stern glare, and walked away.

He knew that the boy would most likely recover the spear and either use it successfully against an Aquilonian or die in the attempt. Either way, another life or two didn't make much difference in the overall scheme of things. More important by far to get to Cuirn and try to get him to surrender to the Aquilonians.

No one stood between Invictus and his goal. Cuirn's hut was, as yet, undamaged. The doorway faced the other direction, and Invictus couldn't tell from where he was whether there was anyone inside, or if perhaps Cuirn had fallen elsewhere in the battle. Invictus hurried across the unspoiled ground, tendrils of smoke drifting toward him from behind. At the hut's back wall, he stopped, listened. Heard nothing. Biting back his anxiety, he went around to the opening, blocked by a single animal skin drapery.

"Cuirn," he called in his rough Pictish. "It is Invictus!" He drew back the skin as he spoke, and went inside.

Cuirn huddled at the back of the large open space, shivering as if from intense cold. He had to have seen sixty years, if not more, and was wrinkled and frail, incredibly old for a Pict, who seldom lived beyond the early forties.

"Invictus?" he said, his voice quavering. He drew long gray hair away from his face and blinked several times. Eagle feathers were tied to it, drooping behind him. Invictus knew that he stood silhouetted in the doorway, so he entered farther and let the skin fall into place behind him.

"Yes, it's me, Cuirn," he said.

"They're . . . they're killing us all." Cuirn looked thin and pale, worse than Invictus had ever seen him. Usually, the old man wore his age well, remaining physically active in spite of his advanced years. But even though it had only been a few months since Invictus had seen him, he seemed to have aged decades, as if he had reached his eighties in that short span of time. "Why?"

"I don't know, Cuirn," Invictus said. It was the simple truth. "I was away from Koronaka when the plans were laid."

"Can't you stop it?" the old man asked. "The pain . . . I feel it all."

Cuirn was a powerful shaman, Invictus knew. Like all of his kind, he indulged often in figurative speaking. But he was not given to hyperbole, so if he claimed that he felt the pain of his clan, it was just possible that he meant it literally. Invictus knew the old man had powers beyond those of mere mortals. That, at least, would explain his appearance, drawn and pale. His lower lip shook like an aspen in a high wind, and his head was nodding manically.

"I'm sorry, Cuirn," Invictus said, meaning it. "I can save you, and perhaps a few others. But the rest—it's out of my hands. If the clan surrenders now, then maybe . . ."

"I . . . I trusted you, Invictus." The old man's feeble muttering sliced to Invictus's heart, as surely as a dagger.

"We were betrayed," Invictus admitted. "Both of us." He hesitated for a moment, not sure what his next move should be. "Can you walk?" he asked. "We should get out of here, gather any we can, and get down the hill."

"It's too late for that," Cuirn said. "Too late for any of it."

"As long as we draw breath it isn't too late to try," Invictus argued.

Before either man could speak again, the skin over the door rustled and was yanked aside.

"You're wrong, brother," Lupinius said as he entered the hut, his sword in his hand. "It is entirely too late."

8

LUPINIUS HAD GUESSED that his brother would lead him to the old shaman, more efficiently than if he had tried to search from hut to hut. He had hung back, giving Invictus plenty of leeway to find the right man. As soon as he had seen Invictus enter the hut on the rim of the hill, he had been sure. The shaman would know where the treasure hoard was kept, if anyone did.

Now, in the dim light of the hut's shadowed interior, looking at the wizened old creature who shivered on the floor and pleaded with Invictus, he knew he had been right again.

Invictus turned to face Lupinius, his face a mask of undisguised anger and contempt. Good to know his brother's true feelings, for once. The man had become such a diplomat that it was often hard to tell where he stood. "Lupinius," he said. "What is the meaning of this wholesale slaughter?"

"I already told you, Invictus," Lupinius replied calmly. "We need to send an unmistakable message to these savages."

"That message is more than clear, I believe," Invictus said. "Now call off your dogs. Spare these people any further outrage."

"We can spare this one," Lupinius said, pointing toward the old shaman with the point of his sword, "if he'll tell me what I want to know."

"If you think I'm going to let you interrogate Cuirn, you—"

Lupinius silenced his brother with a sudden thrust of his blade into the other's throat, just above the mailed shirt and below the helmet. Invictus made a gurgling sound and dropped his own sword, both hands leaping to his neck as if he could contain the blood that already gushed forth from the wound. The look in his eyes was one of absolute surprise. He had probably never guessed that his own brother would slit his throat one day. For Lupinius's part, he had assumed since his eleventh year that he'd have to do it eventually.

The old man watched in horror as Invictus slowly slumped to the hard-packed dirt floor of his hut, his blood pooling beneath him.

"He . . . he is your brother?" the shaman asked in broken Aquilonian.

"He was," Lupinius corrected. "Apparently I am an only child now."

"Why did you . . . ?"

"He was in my way," Lupinius explained. "And about to be more so. You have information I need, and he did not want me to have it."

The old man pressed his hands against the back of the hut and forced himself to his feet. He was a good foot shorter than Lupinius, maybe a little more. His gray hair was thin and wispy, floating in an erratic halo around his shaking head.

"I know what you seek," the old man said, his voice sounding somehow more authoritative than it had just moments ago. "But you will not have it."

"I will," Lupinius argued. "Unless you want to join your fellow savages in the Mountains of the Dead."

"Better that than betray my sacred trust," the shaman replied.

Lupinius shook his head. "I fail to understand that kind of thinking."

"That, sadly, does not surprise me at all," the shaman said.

"You know where it is. I want it. Just tell me where to find it, and I will call off my troops. You'll live, and so will many of your clan."

"Even if you found it, it would not bring you what you think it would," the shaman said. "Give up now before it is too late for you. Go home."

"I will go home when I have the hoard in my possession, and not before, you old fool," Lupinius said with a snarl. "This is your last chance to save yourself."

"No." The shaman looked Lupinius right in the eye. "It is yours."

Lupinius lost all patience with the ancient man. He would speak in riddles, but he couldn't bring himself to answer a simple request. Lupinius raised his sword as high as he could in the small space and brought it down at an angle, slicing through the shaman's neck. His head spun across the hut, bounced off the far wall, then fell to the floor. Finally, it came to rest, sitting up on its stump, eyes open as if regarding Lupinius even in death. His body had slumped backward against the wall, then fallen over sideways.

Before Lupinius could leave the hut, the eyes blinked once, and the ancient, wrinkled mouth moved. "You think you know what you seek," the head said. "But you are sadly mistaken. Not as sad as you will be if you find it, however."

Lupinius recoiled in horror from the unnatural thing, then, scowling, he kicked dirt at the head and hurried from the hut before it could speak again.

Outside, the sounds of battle were dying out. Even the

keening of the Pictish women had largely stopped, as most of them were dead. Smoke grayed the sky, blotting out the sun overhead. Rangers moved from body to body, looting anything that seemed valuable, making sure that the wounded were killed. The Aquilonian soldiers seemed less anxious to participate in these activities, but Lupinius had told his Rangers what he wanted from them, and they did as they were instructed.

The whole scene warmed Lupinius's heart. He almost wished his brother had lived to appreciate it. But then, he wouldn't have, and his complaining would have soured it for Lupinius.

But he still didn't know where the hoard was, and there were precious few Picts still alive who might have been able to tell him. His men could spend a week digging through the ashes of all the burned huts. Even then, it could be cached somewhere out in the surrounding forest, and they'd never find it. He moved from hut to hut, trying to glance inside them despite the flames, when he was summoned by one of his Rangers.

"Lupinius!" It was Trey, a Bossonian he had employed for several months.

"What is it?" he asked.

"Over here!" Trey waved him over to where he stood, at the far edge of the hilltop, not too far from the shaman's hut. He pointed down the hill with his bow. Lupinius had to lean out to look down and see what he indicated.

A dozen feet below the top of the hill, bushes mostly obscured an opening in the ground. From the bottom of the hill, on the west side, no one would ever have known there was an opening there. But from the top of the hill— where normally none but a Pict would stand—it was clear that the bushes only masked a large hole in the ground. Pictish bodies lay in a pile around it.

"A torch!" Lupinius shouted excitedly. Suddenly, he was convinced that the cave was the location of the hoard.

He held out his left hand, and after a few moments someone put a torch into it. With that in his left and his sword in his right, he scrambled down the steep slope to the opening. "Get these bushes out of my way!" he demanded.

A couple of Rangers slid down the slope and chopped at the bushes with axe and sword, tugging them away from the cave's mouth. Now that Lupinius could see inside, he was even more convinced that he had stumbled upon his goal. The cave was deep—he could only see a few feet into it from here, so he guessed it curved just a short way in. And it looked out of place on the slope, as if it had been dug by hand instead of occurring here naturally. The ceiling, walls, and floor were of the same granite as the hilltop itself, which would have made digging it out a complicated, difficult process.

But it could have been done, if someone had had something that he very much wanted to hide.

Lupinius shouldered past the Rangers and into the opening. He had to crouch a little to go in, walking in a kind of sideways, crablike manner, the torch thrust out before him and his sword alongside. For the first few feet, the way was clear, the walls surprisingly clean, as if even the spiders and rats knew to keep away from the place. Then, as he had suspected, the cave's passageway hooked sharply to the left. He followed it. Darkness engulfed him as he moved away from the mouth, only his torch keeping it at bay. He began to see strange markings on the walls, red and blue and black representations of natural things—animals, mountains, the sun, the stars, a river. But mixed in with these were others that he couldn't recognize—a creature that seemed to loom over a mountain like some gargantuan bird, but with ten legs and what appeared to be a long trunk, another that appeared to slither like a snake, but with a fanged head at each end and arms in the middle, and more. Lupinius shivered. First that talking head, now these bizarre images. He didn't like any of this supernatural nonsense.

He tried to ignore the markings on the walls and concentrate on what waited ahead of him. Untold riches, according to the rumors. Gold and jewels that the Picts had stored for centuries—dug from the earth or stolen from travelers, but with no value to those barbaric people. He had even heard that the hoard had been started because the bones of one of their ancient wise men had turned into gold, after the man's death—a solid gold skeleton, with sapphire eyes and ruby teeth. Probably just a story, but with these savages, one never knew. Enough wealth, according to the whispers, to buy him real power.

The torch flickered as if from a sudden wind. For one horrific moment Lupinius thought it would go out. But it didn't. Instead, it roared back to life and illuminated, momentarily, what appeared to be a chamber at the end of the tunnel. Lupinius nervously hurried toward it, the charred wood of his flickering torch providing the only real smell in the cave's stale air.

His first instinct had been correct. It *was* a chamber, a vast room with a ceiling that disappeared in blackness that the torch's glow couldn't penetrate. The walls had been marked over years—centuries, probably—by torches, by pigment, by tools chiseling pictures into them, so much so that the images were layered thickly over one another so that Lupinius couldn't make out any of them.

He didn't waste much effort trying, however, because his attention was riveted on something else.

Near the center of the chamber was a kind of pedestal that looked as if it had been formed of the stuff of the cave itself, like a stalagmite that had been cut off chest high. Blackened human skulls were piled around its base. The weird pedestal glowed with some strange internal luminescence, a soft greenish light that bathed the object that rested on its flat surface.

On top of it, all by itself, as if on display, was a crown.

It was nothing fancy, though easily identifiable for what it was. A circle of aged, brown bones, connected with copper, with an opening for a head. The thing was decorated with enormous, sharp teeth. Lupinius didn't know what they were from, could hardly imagine an animal with a mouth big enough to accommodate them. From the general shape he believed they had belonged to a mammal of some kind, not one of the great oceanic predators he'd heard about.

The crown was a barbarous-looking thing, primitive, of course, but somehow he had a sense of great power as he looked at it. The thing made him uncomfortable. At the same time, he knew it had to have value. The shaman's talking head, the cave, the weird light . . . all indicated that this was an item of great import to the Picts. He hadn't found a hoard of any kind, but perhaps this was the treasure that had been whispered of.

At any rate, it was here before him, and unguarded. He stepped toward it, reached for it.

"Stop," a voice commanded in Pictish. Lupinius didn't know much of the language, but he'd been on the border enough to learn some. "That is not for you."

Lupinius halted in his tracks, tried to suppress a shiver. He had seen no other person since entering the cave, much less within the chamber. But now a man stepped from the shadows behind the pedestal and plucked the crown from it, putting the bizarre ornament on his own head.

If the shaman in the hut above had been old, then this man was positively ancient. Long strands of thin silver hair hung in thatches from his head, like tufts of grass sticking out of an otherwise bare desert landscape. His pale, gray flesh looked paper-thin, and even in the torchlight Lupinius could see blue veins beneath it. He was so frail and stick-thin that Lupinius was amazed that his legs could support his body, or his neck hold his head upright. The fact that his voice carried such authority was frankly amazing. He wore a tunic that had deteriorated until it was little more than a few strips of rotting fabric hanging from his frame, and he carried no weapons that Lupinius could see. His bulging eyes blinked rapidly in the torchlight.

Lupinius raised his sword so the ancient one could see it. "Are you going to stop me?"

The man stepped closer. Lupinius could tell that he didn't like the torchlight—he had probably spent so many years here in the dark that it nearly blinded him. But he came on nonetheless, his hands hooking into jagged-nailed claws. Lupinius could smell his acrid stench over the torch's smoke.

"If you do not leave," the man warned, "you will regret it." His threat reminded Lupinius of the shaman's. So many empty words, spoken by men too old to back up their promises with action. The magic he had already seen was the only aspect of this that gave him pause. But he had come this far . . .

Setting the torch on the bare stone floor, Lupinius reached for the crown. "You do not frighten me, old man," he said. "I'll just take the thing from your head instead of from its resting spot."

As soon as he spoke, the old man rushed him. Lupinius lifted his blade, but in the dark the man evaded it. He dug his deep clawed hands into Lupinius's upper arm and neck. Pain shot through Lupinius, and he wondered if the ancient one's fingernails carried some kind of poison. He released the crown and smashed his left fist into the old man's face. Lupinius heard a grunt of pain, but the man didn't release him.

The sword was useless at such close quarters. Lupinius opened his hand. The weapon fell with a clatter to the rock floor. He tried to pry the old man loose with both hands, but the Pict only increased his grip, his powerful claws tearing agonizingly into Lupinius's flesh. Lupinius felt his own blood running down his chest and arm and knew that if he couldn't shake the strange old man off, he would fall eventually from loss of blood.

A thought struck him. He risked destroying the crown, but at that point it would be a small price to pay to rid himself of the oversized leech clinging to him. He hurled himself toward the stony pedestal, with the old man between him and it.

They slammed into the pedestal with such force that Lupinius heard the crunch of bone over the old man's pained wailing. The old man's horrible grip released partially, and Lupinius drew back and plowed into the pedestal again, grinding the old one between. The man let out another cry of pain, but Lupinius kept up the pressure. Finally, the old man's claws released him altogether.

Lupinius shoved the Pict away from him and scooped up his sword. The ancient one crouched, curled and broken, on the floor, not far from the guttering torch. The weird crown still ornamented his head, but he didn't look like royalty—just like a half-blind man who had taken incredible punishment and yet somehow clung to life.

Not for long. Lupinius drew himself to his full height, ignoring his wounds and the blood that dried on him, and swung his long blade, slicing through the old man's withered neck. Head and crown thumped to the floor. For a moment, Lupinius was afraid this head, like the shaman's, would start talking to him.

It didn't.

He gave it a minute, just to be sure. The head was silent, wide, bulging eyes staring into the darkness above, unblinking at last. Then, before Lupinius's startled eyes, it began to shrink in on itself, to wither, as if all the years the old man had lived were suddenly catching up to him all at once. The man's flesh rotted from his bones, which themselves crumbled to dust, and the dust itself formed into wormlike patterns that slithered away into minute crevices in the earth. Less than a minute from when he had slain the man, there was no sign in the chamber that he had ever existed. Fighting back his disgust at the unnatural, Lupinius lifted the strange crown from the bare dirt on which it now rested.

If this was the only treasure he would realize from this adventure, so be it. There was always a place to sell magical objects like the crown. He would take whatever he could get.

9

ALANYA COULDN'T BELIEVE what she was hearing.

She had feared the worst, watching the column of soldiers returning from their raid on the Bear Clan village and not seeing her father among them. Finally, she saw him, but laid across his saddle like downed game, not sitting upright like the man that he was. She heard Donial gasp beside her and knew that he had seen it, too.

She ran to the column then, her eyes filling with tears, and a couple of Lupinius's Rangers saw her coming and blocked her way. They grabbed her arms and wrestled her to the side as the column continued riding into the fort and toward the parade ground. One of the Rangers tried to whisper reassuringly, but Alanya could only hear the rush of blood in her ears and the steady drumming of hooves on solid earth.

Now, an hour later, she and Donial were in Lupinius's study. Their uncle had poured them each a mug of wine, and when he spoke, his voice was steady and sympathetic. "I know this will be a hard time for you," he said. "Hard for all of us. You love your father, as I love my brother. But he has been taken from us, and we all will need to rely on each other instead."

"Can you tell us how it happened, Uncle?" Donial asked. That was just like him, Alanya thought disgustedly. His father was dead, and he wanted the horrific details. As if he weren't the one ultimately responsible.

Lupinius seemed to understand how she felt and spared them the worst of it. "Your father fought bravely and well," he said. "The Picts gave a savage defense, and many of us fell to them. But Invictus fought ferociously, and a number of the enemy died beneath his sword. Finally, though, he was battling the village's shaman, a very powerful sorcerer. The shaman held him off with barbarous magic until several other Picts could surround him. I tried to offer aid, but was busy fighting through half a dozen myself. Before I could reach him, I saw him fall to their attacks. Courageous to the end, the ground around him was littered with Pict bodies."

Donial looked like he took some solace from that description, but Alanya didn't believe it. Her father had respected the Picts, and especially their holy men. She had heard him speak of the Bear Clan shaman as if he were an old friend. He would have been trying to stop the battle, not trying to kill them.

"But we were victorious in the end, right?" Donial asked. *We,* as if he had been there himself, Alanya noted, fighting alongside them.

"Of course," Lupinius said. His tone of voice made it seem a foregone conclusion. "The Bear Clan is no more. They will never trouble Aquilonia again."

She shivered at Donial's visible delight. His smile grew wide, his eyes sparkling. But then another terrible thought gripped her. Her shiver became more pronounced.

If the Bear Clan was completely wiped out, then what of Kral? Him, too? She couldn't come out and ask

Lupinius. It had been her meetings with Kral, after all, that had prompted the raid in the first place. "No survivors?" she asked, hoping the question was vague enough not to arouse suspicion.

"No survivors," Lupinius confirmed, with a self-satisfied light in his dark eyes. "Our forces were very efficient."

He talked on, mostly answering Donial's probing questions about the battle, but Alanya barely heard. Her father and her new friend, both killed in a conflict of which she had been the cause. Tears welled in her eyes once again, and she sat silently, her hands pressed into fists so tight that her own fingernails dug into her, until Lupinius excused them both.

DONIAL HAD NOT wanted to believe that Lupinius would lie to them. He still didn't, not completely. In the haze of battle, he reasoned, people sometimes made mistakes, or thought they saw things they really didn't.

Trouble was, Alanya was right. She had pointed out that their father knew the Bear Clan shaman and liked him. Given Invictus's charge from King Conan, he would more likely have been trying to negotiate a peace with the shaman than trying to kill him. All of that rang true, and the idea that their father would do battle with a wizened old man, such as he had described the shaman, was beyond the realm of the possible.

It had taken her most of the evening, and lots of shouting and tears, to convince him. But finally she had done so. He had gone to bed that night but barely slept, instead tossing and thinking over the things she had said. In the morning, he had agreed to her request.

Which was why they were waiting together outside the office of Governor Sharzen.

Alanya had put on one of her nicest dresses, long and

green, with a beribboned waistline and hem. Her blond
hair was pulled back and tied with a red ribbon that matched
those in her dress. She was clean and fresh-looking. She
had persuaded Donial to go to the public bath himself, and
his dark hair was freshly washed, his white tunic clean and
unripped. Alanya said they looked presentable, and that
was the important thing.

They had been waiting for about twenty minutes before
the governor himself opened the door to his inner office
and invited them in. Even a day later, he still looked
flushed with victory, his round cheeks apple red, his blunt
features shining with excitement.

"Welcome, children," he said, rubbing his hands together as he looked at them. Donial was put in mind of an
ogre in a children's story who was preparing to eat two little children—and he didn't like being referred to that way
in the first place, being fourteen and no longer a child. But
to people like Sharzen, he guessed, everyone was a child
until he or she was decidedly adult. Annoying, but there it
was. Donial decided to let it pass.

"Come in," Sharzen added. Donial wished he would
stop rubbing his hands. He looked like he was cold, rubbing them together for friction, or to start a fire. He backed
away from the door, and Donial and Alanya followed
him in.

Donial had been in his office before, but was surprised
once again at how much fancier it was than most places
here on the border. The furniture had all been brought in
from Aquilonia, not hewn from native woods. There were
fine rugs on the floor, and wall hangings, and pillows of the
softest yellow silk to sit on.

Sharzen indicated a couple of piles of pillows, and Donial and Alanya sat with legs crossed. Alanya had agreed
that she would do most of the talking, and she didn't let
Donial down. "Thank you for agreeing to see us, Governor," she began.

"What can I do for you?" Sharzen asked as he lowered himself onto his own stack of pillows. "I hope you know how sorry I am about your father. Still, he went down with his sword arm swinging and his enemies clustered thickly about his feet, a warrior to the end."

"Then you there when he died?" Alanya asked.

Sharzen looked troubled for a moment. "Not right on the spot," he said. "I was directing activity down the slope a bit."

"So you did not actually see him killed," she pressed.

"I heard about it, immediately after," Sharzen hedged. "Lupinius could not stop talking about how brave he was."

"We have heard all about that," Alanya said. Donial had to suppress a smile. "But it seems that Uncle Lupinius was the only witness."

Sharzen seemed to think that over for a moment. "Perhaps, yes. The only one I have heard about it from."

Donial could see his sister steel herself. "We are not convinced that it really happened that way, Governor," she said.

Sharzen looked astonished. "You think your uncle is . . . what, mistaken?"

"Sometimes in battle people get confused," Donial interjected. "Or so I have heard."

"Sometimes," Sharzen admitted with a sage nod. "But in this case . . . I think Lupinius would recognize his own brother."

"Probably he would," Alanya agreed, shooting Donial a look meant to remind him who was supposed to be talking. "But what he describes does not sound like our father," she explained. "He liked the Bear Clan shaman. They were friends."

"That is a strong word—I cannot imagine an Aquilonian and a Pict ever really being friends. Anyway, friendship doesn't always survive war," Sharzen pointed out.

"But we were not at war with the Picts," Alanya said. "In fact, our father was working hard to prevent war. I just cannot imagine him turning into someone who would try to kill his own friend. It isn't his way."

"Even if he saw that shaman trying to perform a spell that would kill many Aquilonians?" Sharzen offered.

"Possibly then," Alanya said. "Was there such a spell?"

"I know not," Sharzen said. "We know there are spells used in war all the time."

"I'm sorry, Governor, but that is not very convincing," Alanya replied. "If there was such a spell, why have there not been other tales of its use by the Picts? Why would my father be the only one who witnessed it?"

"Perhaps not convincing to you," Sharzen said, ignoring her question. He put on sympathy like a mask. "But then, you have lost your father, and I'm not surprised that you would cling to an idealized version of his death."

"We are not . . ." Alanya didn't even finish her sentence. It was clear that Sharzen was dismissing their suspicions, and them. To make it even more apparent, he stood up and folded his muscular arms over his massive chest.

"I'm afraid I am very busy," he told them. "Is there anything else I can help you with?"

Alanya rose, looking to Donial like she was stifling her rage. Her skin had darkened a little, her brow knitted together, and her eyes burned with barely contained fire. For a moment, Donial hoped she would let fly. But she probably knew it would do them no good to antagonize Koronaka's governor—especially with their father gone and no one to protect them except Lupinius, Sharzen's good friend and ally.

No, if they were ever to find out the truth of what had happened in the Bear Clan village, they would have to do it on their own.

KRAL WAS THREE days away from the village when he saw the smudge of smoke on the horizon. He didn't know

what it meant, but guessed it was trouble. Even though he
had not finished his Spirit Trek, he could tell by its location
between two faraway mountain peaks that the smoke came
from the region of the Bear Clan village. He had been
working on setting a trap using vines and sticks, trying to
catch something for dinner, but he abandoned his efforts
and set off at a run.

He covered ground quickly and tirelessly, taking long
strides at an even pace. He had gone into the wilderness
without clothing or weapons, as tradition demanded, so
had no constrictions slowing him down or adding un-
wanted weight. The days were still warm, so the breeze
blowing across him as he ran was welcome.

When night's full darkness came on, he had to stop for
fear of running into a tree—the light of the moon and stars
didn't penetrate the thick forest canopy overhead. He ate
some fruit and berries he found, and allowed himself to
sleep. Before first light, he was up and running again.

At that pace, he swallowed the miles much more
quickly than when he had left at a walk. It was late afternoon on the second day when he reached the village. Since
midmorning, he had feared the worst, as the smoke still
clung to the sky, and it was obvious at last that it came
from the village. A little closer, and he could see swarms of
vultures circling overhead. But it wasn't until he was
wearily climbing the clan's hill, beyond the tree line, that
he knew how bad it really was.

The Bear Clan's village had been burned to the ground.
No hut was more than a smoldering pile of rubble or
scorched mud walls. Bodies lay everywhere—everyone
Kral had ever known, his friends, his neighbors, his aunts
and uncles, mother and father, brother and sisters. Not
even one of the clan's dogs moved among the carnage. The
air was thick with the smell of spilled blood and the
buzzing of flies. The buzzards took wing at Kral's arrival,
but the effect of their work was plain.

Someone had obliterated the entire Bear Clan.

And there was little question who. Even through eyes clouded with grief and fury, Kral saw broken Aquilonian weapons, buckles from belts, pieces of sandal or boot. And there was a path leading from the base of the hill back toward the Black River and Koronaka that a toddler could follow. A Pictish toddler, at any rate.

Unable to stop himself, Kral found his own family's hut—like the rest, a scorched and ruined mess. Blood and the scuff marks of bodies that had been hauled away by the attackers gave a good indication that his people had fought hard and taken many Aquilonian lives.

He had expected no less.

But he should have been here to help. His clan had needed him, and he had been away.

A sudden, terrible thought struck him. The Guardian of the Teeth! It was possible that he, at least, had survived—the Aquilonians had come up the opposite slope, and might not have seen the cave's entrance. Suddenly hopeful, he hurried to the far rim and skidded downhill to the mouth.

Even before he reached it, though, he saw the corpses piled around it and that the bushes guarding it had been butchered. From inside he could smell the alien stench of fire and death—two smells that he had never associated with the cave, as long as he had lived. Swallowing, he went in anyway, finding his way through the familiar dark passage. In the inner chamber he searched for the Guardian, and for that which the Guardian was sworn to protect. He found neither. The Teeth of the Ice Bear, the most sacred relic of the Bear Clan, was gone!

Murdering everyone, putting his village to the torch—those were terrible things, for which someone would pay. Kral swore that even as he made his way from the cave, back into the light of day, into the stink of smoke and slaughter, the incessant drone of the flies, the leathery flap of the vultures' wings.

But taking the Teeth . . . that was a crime compounding the rest, somehow more horrible because it was clearly not an act of war, just the most base kind of thievery. Someone had the Teeth; someone had stolen it.

"That someone will pay," Kral declared aloud. "This I vow!"

10

THE FUNERAL WAS held the next day.

Ordinarily, their father's social rank would mean that his body would lie in state for several days, while people he knew, and family members, visited to show their respect for him. In Tarantia, that might have happened.

Here in the Westermarck, however, Donial understood that things were different. Their father had no relatives besides them and Lupinius. And he had not died alone, but in the company of a couple dozen soldiers. All of their bodies had been brought back to Koronaka by the invading force. Rather than allow them to sit out in the early-autumn heat, they were to be cremated immediately, on a group pyre just outside the fort's walls.

So his body was one of many, laid out on the parade ground where, just days before, soldiers had drilled for the attack. Donial and Alanya went to see him one last time. Standing before his father's lifeless form, Donial felt his knees grow weak. Alanya's hand was suddenly in his, clutching it tightly.

A mixture of powerful emotions coursed through Donial. He believed himself to bear much of the responsibility for his father's death. If he had not told what he saw in the forest that day, none of these things would have happened. But fault belonged to Alanya as well. She was the one who had carried on a secret relationship with a Pictish boy. The fact that both were culpable in some way kept either one from pointing fingers of blame, Donial thought.

None of which helped him feel better about looking at the handsome, empty figure on the platform. Donial loved his father, but perhaps more important, he respected the man. Father had always been hardworking, honest, available to his children. After his wife died, he took on the sole responsibility for raising Donial and Alanya, and he taught them the same virtues by which he lived.

Uncle Lupinius said that their father had asked him to care for them if anything ever happened to him. They had already been staying with Lupinius while Father was gone on his mission, so that would not change.

Alanya sobbed softly at his side. Elsewhere on the parade grounds, people stood silently, or wept openly, or prostrated themselves in the dirt in unabashed sorrow. Donial blinked back his own tears and wished there was something he could say to Alanya. But he didn't trust his own voice. He vaguely remembered their mother's funeral, back in Tarantia, at which he had cried long and loud, then been too choked up for anything resembling normal conversation for days. He was older now, more mature. And with Father gone, he had to carry more of the family's weight. Whether he was ready or not, he had to become a man. He felt like everyone in the town was watching them, knowing it was their fault the raid had happened. So he kept his mouth closed, refused to let the tears fall.

He had heard people say their hearts were broken. He had just never known before exactly what they meant.

While they watched, Alanya still crushing his hand with

both of hers, soldiers started collecting the bodies for the procession to the pyre outside the walls. He could already smell the smoke. The keening of the mourners grew louder. As two soldiers approached Father, Donial's stomach clenched. His face flushed. This would really be farewell. When they lifted him by shoulders and feet—with respect, Donial thought, but still giving the unintended impression that he was nothing now but a heavy piece of meat—one of them said softly to his companion, "Did you see the wound? Looks more like a sword thrust than one of their spears or arrows." They carried the body away before the other replied.

Donial glanced in alarm at his sister, but she didn't seem to have noticed. He would tell her what he had heard—later, when he trusted himself to speak again. It didn't necessarily mean anything. A Pict might have used a sword taken from an Aquilonian corpse. Or the soldier's estimation might have been wrong. Who knew how much experience he had judging such things, or on the field of battle?

Bad enough that he had to mourn his father—did he now have to suspect his uncle of some complicity in the crime? Lupinius, or someone in his employ. Glad now that Alanya held him, Donial felt like the world spun crazily beneath his feet, trying to hurl him off into space.

UNCLE LUPINIUS'S SYMPATHETIC demeanor only lasted through the cremation.

Alanya had hoped that the conversation she and Donial had had with Governor Sharzen would remain private. Apparently, that was not to be. Lupinius went to see the governor the next day, following the funeral, and came back to the house scowling furiously. He did not specifically address the accusation she and Donial had made, but he tossed both of them angry looks and stomped around the place like a petulant child.

After several hours of this behavior, during which Lupinius hadn't had a civil word to say to either of them, Alanya went into Donial's room and closed the door. "He knows what we did," she speculated. "It's the only reason for him to be acting like this."

"Do you think so?" Donial sat cross-legged on some cushions, his dark hair unkempt and falling into his eyes, his long shirt unbelted. He hadn't left the house today. It didn't look like he had any intention of doing so.

"He just took me aside and told me we are restricted to the fort," she reported. "No leaving the walls under any circumstances."

"Not so unreasonable," Donial said. Even now, knowing what he did, or suspecting it, he was willing to defend Lupinius when he could. "The Picts—"

"Are all dead," Alanya interrupted.

"True, I suppose," Donial admitted. "But what if other clans seek revenge?"

"From what I understand, that is not very likely." Alanya went to the window of Donial's room. She looked out, past the barracks toward the log walls that now formed the boundaries of her life. The flames of the cremation pyre seemed almost still visible, as if they had been burned into her eyes. They had leapt high, stark against evening's indigo sky. Governor Sharzen had spoken before the pyre, and Lupinius, and two priests of Mitra who lived at the fort. She couldn't remember a word any of them had said. "They seem to be at war with each other as much as with anyone else."

"So you think he just wants to punish us?"

"If the raid on the Bear Clan eliminated that threat, then it should be safer for us out in the woods than it used to be, not less safe. So either he's wrong about killing all the Picts, or he's just angry with us. He can't be angry with us because our father died—at least, I should not think so. And he was this way when he came back from meeting with Governor Sharzen. So I think Sharzen told him what we feared."

"I guess that makes sense," Donial said.

Alanya did not answer right away, just gazed out the window. Even if she could leave the fort, without Kral out there, she had very little reason to. And now with their father gone and Uncle Lupinius their caretaker, she didn't know when she'd be able to get back home to Tarantia, or what would become of Father's house there. In one day, not only had she lost her only remaining parent, but also any hope of seeing her friends again. Her entire future seemed in doubt. On the frontier there were few opportunities for her. As soon as she was able to get away from here, she would do so, but it was dangerous for a young woman to travel alone. And Donial wasn't yet of an age to be able to escort her.

Her world had been turned inside out, with two huge holes left in her heart by the loss of her father and her friend. Both would heal, in time, she supposed. Until then, she would carry the pain with her everywhere. Being stuck inside Koronaka's four log walls would only make it worse.

"WE NEED A bigger wall."

Lupinius walked with Sharzen along the existing perimeter of Koronaka's walls, glancing up now and then at the parapets from which soldiers stood watch over the forests beyond. His goal of recovering a Pictish treasure hoard having been thwarted for the time being, it looked like he might be staying in the Westermarck a bit longer than anticipated. So he had been casting about for other ways to increase his personal fortune and importance, and further reinforcing the fort was what he had come up with.

He still had the primitive crown, in a wooden box in his home. Fortunately, he had not been stupid enough to tell anyone else he was after a rumored Pictish hoard. Sharzen would have wanted to share it, and his Rangers would have expected some kind of bonus. But he wasn't sure yet just how he was going to sell the thing. As long as he stayed near the border, there was always the chance that some other Pictish clan might pay a ransom for it. Until he was able to get rid of it, however, he needed to be protected from any Picts who might come looking for it. If it was truly the magical artifact he suspected, then the Picts might even unite in search of whoever had taken it. The wall he proposed would serve that purpose as well.

"A taller wall?" Sharzen asked, confused.

"No," Lupinius clarified. "More extensive, I mean. It isn't enough to simply wall off the fort and the town. We should build a wall that spans the entire frontier, confining the Picts to their side."

"But we've eliminated the threat from the Picts," Sharzen said. He still didn't understand, Lupinius knew. But then, it wasn't intelligence that had won him his job.

"Just one clan," Lupinius reminded him. "But there are many others, and they remain a threat to Aquilonians all along the frontier. If we built a wall that hemmed them all in, kept them penned into their specific area, it would make all of us safer."

He lowered his voice conspiratorially, though he didn't see anyone else close enough to listen in. "Besides, if we—you and I—are the prime movers behind building the wall, then we become two of the most important men in the region, overnight. We are taking steps to ensure the safety of everyone in the border region. We control the building crews and the finances. We can probably get assistance from Aquilonia for such an ambitious project—especially important now that the Picts have broken the truce here and killed King Conan's personal ambassador. Has an emissary gone to the king yet, to let him know of Invictus's tragic demise?"

"He leaves today," Sharzen said. "Now that the funeral rites are over."

"Then he can carry two messages."

Sharzen was beginning to smile, finally catching up with Lupinius's thought processes. "I think I see your point," he said. "And I believe your plan has a lot of merit."

Of course it does, Lupinius thought. He didn't bother to say it, though. Before long, he would have Sharzen thinking the idea had been his own all along. He didn't care which one of them got the credit for coming up with it—he would be too busy counting his gold and enjoying the fruits of his new celebrity for that.

Maybe it should even be called Lupinius's Wall. No, Invictus's Wall. The irony was too delicious to resist . . .

THERE WASN'T MUCH Kral could do for his people now. Their spirits had gone to the Mountains of the Dead. He could build a huge pyre to cremate all the bodies, but that would just create a new column of smoke, like the one drifting over Koronaka, and reveal to any observers that there was still someone alive in the Bear Clan village. That would not suit his ends at all.

So he mourned privately, camped at the base of the hill, and let the insects and birds do their nasty work in the village. He made periodic trips up to the top to gather supplies he might need, including weapons, and as many dark-colored animal skins as he could find. He was putting together the basics of a plan. He just hadn't worked out all the details yet.

Thoughts of Alanya kept creeping unbidden into his mind as he worked. She was no warrior, and certainly hadn't participated in the raid. But if she had known about it, she hadn't warned him. He couldn't tell how long before he had seen the smoke the battle had occurred, but there couldn't have been very much time between his last meeting

with Alanya in the forest clearing and the attack itself. Kral
didn't know much about the Aquilonians' ways of war, but
it seemed as if there must have been time needed for preparation, for beating the drums of war and singing the songs
that would guide departed souls to their resting place.
Could it be that Alanya was ignorant of all that, or did she
simply choose not to tell him?

He did not consider her an enemy. But she was an
Aquilonian, and the Aquilonian people had become his enemies. He didn't anticipate that they would be meeting in
her clearing in the woods again, and wasn't sure what he'd
do if they met in any other place.

The third day after his return, Kral heard someone moving through the nearby forest. He could tell the difference
between animals and humans, and these sounds were definitely human. And there were more than one, though they
were trying very hard to be silent.

Grabbing a bow and some arrows from his cache, he
moved into a nearby stand of pines. There he stood mo-
tionless, waiting and watching. A few minutes passed, then
he saw two people emerge from the trees and start up the
hill toward the village.

Kral was amazed. He recognized them both—Mang,
one of the village's elders, and Klea, one of its women.
Mang had seen nearly fifty years, and while his hair had
grayed, he still stood tall and had the musculature of a
much younger man. Klea was lean and short, not much
over four feet, but she laughed easily and was popular
around campfires at night. Kral emerged from his hiding
place and shouted their names.

"Kral?" Klea said when she saw him. "What happened
here?"

Kral sped up the hill to accompany them to the horrific
scene above. "Aquilonians, from Koronaka," he explained. "I
was away on my Spirit Trek, but saw the smoke and returned,

only too late to fight. This is what I found. I had thought you both dead with everyone else."

"I was hunting, far to the north," Mang explained. "And Klea had gone to bury Eltha, the daughter who died a few days before. We ran into one another yesterday, as we were both returning to the village."

"There is much more burying to be done," Kral suggested. "I had decided not to bother—to leave the corpses here as a testament to the battle our people fought. To burn them would only alert the Aquilonians that their effort had failed, that some of us yet lived, and to bury them all would be too much work."

Tears streamed down Klea's face as she turned to him. Mang tried hard to keep his emotions in check, but his lips quivered, and his eyes looked sorrowful. "Then . . . all the rest are . . . ?" He left the question unfinished.

"Yes," Kral told them. "As far as I can tell. There may be others like you and me, who were away from the village. But certainly most, if not all, are dead."

"Then . . . we are truly without a clan," Klea said, between sobs.

"Or we *are* the clan," Mang observed. "Bad enough they destroy the forests that give us life, now they take away what life we can still claim."

"The Teeth of the Ice Bear is gone as well," Kral reported, hesitant to deliver yet more bad news. "They took it."

Mang's face blanched even more. "They . . ."

"I will get it back," Kral said. "I have already vowed to do so. I was working on my plan when I heard you approach."

"We are not much of a clan," Klea admitted. "But the Teeth remains our responsibility, and an awesome one it is."

"Now that it's gone," Mang said, "it is no longer just our problem. All the Pict clans must be told. They must work with us to return it to its proper home."

"Let them know we failed to protect it?" Klea asked.

"Better they learn it from us than from some horrible event," Mang suggested.

"What horrible event?" Kral wondered. "What magic does the Teeth have sway over?"

Mang and Klea glanced at each other, as if daring the other to answer. Finally, Mang spoke up. "None of us are entirely sure," he said. "I have heard many guesses, but no one seemed to know exactly what."

"So we've spent generations protecting it, and we don't even know *why*?" Kral asked.

"Perhaps the Guardian did," Klea guessed. "But it is too late to ask him now."

"Too late to ask anyone," Kral grouched.

"The Teeth of the Ice Bear is not merely a Bear Clan superstition," Mang insisted. "Other clans will know of it. All know how important it is to keep safe and protected."

"But they entrusted the Bear Clan with its care," Klea pointed out. "If we tell them that we failed, they will kill us as likely as aid us."

"We have no choice," Mang said. "We don't know what might happen with the Teeth gone. We need to warn the other clans. At the same time, we should try to unite them against Aquilonia. This was not just an attack against the Bear Clan, this was an attack against all Picts. It needs to be treated as such, and the proper response made."

"Unite?" Klea spat on the scorched earth. "The clans have never united, even against a common enemy. They aren't likely to start now."

"Not if we do not try," Mang countered adamantly. "But the Teeth has never gone missing before. And there's never been a massacre like this to demonstrate how real the threat is. If we do not unite, the Aquilonians will pick us off, clan by clan. United, we can make them pay, and drive them back across the Thunder River again, out of our territory for good."

Klea smiled. "I would love to believe you," she said. "I am not convinced, but I am willing to try."

Kral was surprised at the turn the conversation was taking. He had believed as Klea did, that nothing could unite the clans. But he had his own ideas about how to get the Teeth back and at the same time exact the appropriate revenge against the Aquilonians, and it didn't involve having to explain his actions to the others.

"Perhaps the two of you should go to them," he suggested. "Approach the other clans, tell them what has transpired here, warn them that the Teeth is out of our care for now. We only need a temporary truce of the clans, so they can work together against our common enemies. I will stay here and try to learn what I can from the settlers at Koronaka."

"Learn how?" Klea inquired.

"I have some ideas," Kral said simply. That was as much as he wanted to reveal at present.

"Very well," Mang said. He took a look around the wasted village, the corpses strewn everywhere. "Fix this in your mind, Klea, so we can describe the scene to the others. Every Pict must know the atrocities of which the Aquilonians are capable."

Kral didn't think that part would be hard. He would never be able to rid himself of the image of his village after the soldiers had left it, no matter how many years he lived. Some things one couldn't forget.

Or forgive.

11

KELAN WAS GLAD that Rossun stood watch with him that night.

One regular army soldier and one Ranger on every shift, that was the new rule. Rumor said it was something about making sure that everyone remembered Lupinius's role in the whole wall project. Kelan paid scant attention to rumors, nor did he much care what the reasoning was. He just didn't want to be out here alone.

Work on the wall had only been under way for five days. But in those five days, not a single night had gone by without incident. The first night, most of the first day's work was undone. Stones were toppled over before mortar had set, logs knocked askew, tools stolen. The same had happened the next night, and the next, even though guards had been posted. Obviously, someone didn't want the wall built. In five days, only two days' worth of real progress had been made.

So the guards had been doubled. Sharzen and Lupinius were adamant that their wall would be built, and immediately, without waiting for assistance from Tarantia. Again, there were rumors, these suggesting that they wanted to be well along before King Conan heard about the wall, to make it less likely that he would forbid its construction.

So far, the night had been quiet. Kelan was nervous, though; each new wind that rustled tree branches made him start and stare off into the dark. There was almost no moon tonight, and the stars glimmered overhead like cold, far-away chips of ice. The light from the couple of torches they'd jammed into the wall hardly penetrated the night. "You think anything will happen tonight?" he asked Rossun.

"Has every other night," Rossun said, with a shrug. "Our job to find out who is doing it and stop him."

"What if it is not a man at all?" Kelan asked. "What if it's . . . I know not . . ."

"What, some kind of monster?" Rossun returned, with a grin. "Then we kill a monster."

Which didn't exactly fill Kelan with confidence. Killing a monster sounded hard, and dangerous. He'd rather it was vandals from the town. Even Picts, though since the destruction of the Bear Clan that was unlikely.

Rossun pointed down the wall to the left, away from the fort. It was waist high so far, three-quarters of a mile long. This first section had been started about a quarter mile from the fort itself, on a clear, level field. While work progressed here, another crew was busily cutting trees to make way for the wall closer to Koronaka. But at night, Kelan couldn't even see Koronaka's lights from his post. "Why don't you walk down to that end?" Rossun suggested. "I'll go to the other, then we'll turn around and walk back toward each other, you on this side of the wall and me on the other. When we meet, we'll continue to the other man's end and reverse. That way we'll cover most of the wall every few minutes instead of leaving large parts of it totally unguarded."

"Sounds good to me," Kelan said, although it didn't. He didn't want to admit to Rossun how anxious he was about being alone. There was something very wrong about the whole thing, and he just couldn't decide what it was. So he agreed with Rossun and nervously began walking toward his end of the wall, trying to peer through the nearly absolute darkness with every step.

As he walked, he turned every now and again to look back at Rossun, reassuring himself that his comrade was still there. When he was looking forward, the whistle of the wind swept away the sound of Rossun's footsteps, and he might as well have been completely alone. He loosed his short sword in its scabbard, just in case—though what good it would be against a monster he wasn't sure.

He heard his own feet crunching against earth packed hard by the weight of men carrying heavy rocks for the wall's base, snapping the occasional twig that had blown there. He heard the wind. He heard the mournful cry of some hidden night bird.

He was almost to the end of the wall when he heard another sound, so out of place it made the hairs on the back of his neck stand up. It was the steady, rhythmic sound of someone breathing.

And it was right on the other side of the wall.

He looked, but didn't see anyone there. He glanced back toward Rossun, whose back was to him, almost to his own end of the wall. He could call for him, but didn't want the Ranger to think he was a coward, crying out at the first odd sound.

Instead, he slipped his sword from its scabbard, took a deep breath, and leaned over the wall.

And squatting there, looking up at him, was a young Pict with a long dagger in his fist, his face and torso painted as blue as the night sky.

Kelan raised his sword to swing and tried to find his voice at the same time. But the Pict was faster, and he drove up with the dagger before Kelan could even bring his sword into position. The point of the Pict's knife slammed into Kelan's mail shirt with enough force to knock Kelan over backward. He landed on his back, the sword still clutched in his fist. Before he could push himself upright, the Pict charged over the wall at him.

This time, Kelan was able to react quickly enough, blocking the Pict's advance with the short sword. The Pict corrected his attack midstride, ducking away from the sword. He moved silently, eyes never leaving Kelan's face, lips compressed in a tight but unmistakable smile.

"Where is the crown?" the Pict asked quietly, in heavily accented Aquilonian.

"Crown? I don't know what you're talking about."

"You get no second chance," the Pict whispered.

"Rossun!" Kelan called, no longer worried about being thought a coward.

As he did, however, he glanced toward where the Ranger should be. The Pict took advantage of the momentary lapse in concentration and dodged around the short sword. When Kelan looked back, the Pictish youth was right there in front of his face, the smile now broad and satisfied. He still held the dagger, but his other hand was cupped, as if holding something precious. He blew into his palm, and a fine dark powder blasted Kelan's face. Kelan felt a burning pain in his eyes, then in his lungs. He dropped his sword. The darkness of the night seemed to wrap around him like a shroud, then it enveloped him completely.

ROSSUN THOUGHT HE heard his name. But the wind snatched sound away almost before it could travel even a few feet, so he wasn't sure. He turned, just the same. Couldn't see Kelan anywhere.

Just in case, he drew his sword and ran down the wall toward where Kelan should have been. A few moments later, he saw the soldier on the ground, seven or eight feet from the wall. He looked like he was curled up and taking a nap.

But when he reached Kelan he discovered that wasn't the case at all. His eyes were wide-open, bulging visibly from his skull. His mouth was twisted in a horribly pained expression, blood trickling from both corners of his mouth. Rossun knelt beside him. "Who did this?" he asked. "Kelan, did you see who it was?"

Kelan didn't answer, and after a couple of minutes he ceased to move at all.

Rossun swallowed hard. Someone—or some*thing*—had murdered Kelan, just a short distance away from him. He hadn't seen any sign of the killer, hadn't heard the struggle. He'd been facing the wrong way, and the wind didn't let sound travel far. But still, he should have been aware that something was going on.

He stood up carefully, his sword at the ready. Whoever had killed Kelan couldn't be far away yet. There was every chance he was still nearby, in the dark, watching Rossun. Maybe getting ready to attack even now.

Nervously, Rossun turned in a slow circle, trying to penetrate the blackness with his gaze. He saw nothing, no one. Whoever had murdered Kelan had faded immediately into the shadows.

No way to track the killer now. It was too dark, and he'd as likely wander off in the wrong direction altogether as actually find the killer's tracks. The dirt was full of footprints from the workers coming and going.

Instead, he decided he should return to Koronaka to sound the alarm.

There was definitely someone working against the wall project, and that someone had just taken his opposition a step further.

A SHORT WHILE later, Kral hurried through the night woods, back toward the Black River and home. He had killed before, in the frenzy of battle, but he had never killed a man so cold-bloodedly. It was a strange sensation—at the same time easier than he'd expected and more difficult. Easy, because the man had barely put up a fight. He had been terrified, shaking so hard he could barely hold his sword. His voice had been a pained squeak.

It had been a simple matter for Kral to use the powdered calera root that Cuirn had taught him about. On the dead, it was used to help with the process of loosening flesh from skulls, for the souvenirs of war many Picts liked to take. But Cuirn had told him that it was also useful for killing, silently and without visible wounds. He had been right— the soldier had collapsed almost instantly, his face contorting terribly.

The killing had been easy, also, because Kral was spurred on by his memories of his own home village, of the things the Aquilonians of Koronaka had done to his family and friends.

And yet, difficult, too, because even though an Aquilonian, the man was still a human being. Thoughts of his friends and neighbors back in the village reminded Kral of the other man's essential humanity—of the fact that he was somebody's son, possibly someone else's father or brother, husband or lover. Kral had no problem thinking of himself as a warrior, and if his clan hadn't been at peace with the settlers of Koronaka, it was likely he'd have already done much more killing.

But a warrior and a murderer were two different things.

He was doing a warrior's work, to be sure. He was trying to find the Teeth of the Ice Bear, and he had to do whatever that task required. But he was using a murderer's methods.

The Aquilonians probably thought him a savage who wouldn't understand such fine distinctions. The truth was, the distinction was important to Picts, who believed that sending enemies to the lands of the dead in the course of battle was one of the noblest things they could ever hope to

do. But killing someone by stealth, without a fair fight—
that was the work of an assassin, not a warrior. He was glad
that his victim had at least tried to fight back.

He hoped they all would, because he suspected there
would be a lot more killing before he found what he was
looking for.

12

IN THE MORNING, Lupinius and Sharzen went to the wall to survey the damage. When Rossun had run back to Koronaka to rouse the troops, someone—presumably, whoever had killed Kelan—had knocked over a large section of the wall.

"He's like a ghost," Lupinius complained. "Rossun saw no one. He says he thought he heard Kelan call out for him, but he turned around and could not see Kelan. By the time he found Kelan, the man was dead. Then he couldn't see the killer, so he came back to Koronaka. At which time, whoever this is, this so-called ghost, did the damage to our wall."

"Does it not seem counter to our goal, to have the building of this wall become a losing struggle instead of a victory?" Sharzen asked.

"We are only just finding that we have an enemy," Lupinius replied. "We can defeat him, whoever he is. Ghost or man. We will put more guards on the wall. We need to get it done. If we abandoned it now, we would look like fools."

"Perhaps it's a foolish idea," Sharzen offered.

"You have never had a foolish idea," Lupinius insisted. "It's a fine idea, and we will make it happen. We simply need more guards at night. Whoever killed Kelan will not dare try anything if there are ten soldiers on the wall, instead of two."

Sharzen studied the pile of rubble, where the rocks mortared into place had been shoved over before the mortar set. "And as the wall grows longer," he said. "Then we will need more. Ten guards every mile? Every half mile? What is the magic number, Lupinius?"

"We need no magic to defeat this ghost, Governor," Lupinius replied. "I am convinced we are being troubled by a man, not a spirit of any kind. We only need to catch him once and kill him. Then the rest of the project will proceed without incident."

Sharzen nodded, but he didn't look convinced. He put his hands on his hips and glared directly at the other man, in a more confrontational manner than he usually did. Lupinius was proud of the way he had learned to manipulate the governor, and hoped the man wasn't suddenly growing a backbone after all this time. "If you say so, Lupinius."

"Of course I do," Lupinius said. He was not as confident as he tried to sound. What if it was the Picts, looking for their crown? What if the theft of the bizarre headgear had summoned some sort of demon? But he couldn't let on to Sharzen, or allow anyone to believe that the crown was more than a simple curiosity. "Look, it cannot be more than one or two of them, or they would have been seen and heard by now. Someone out there does not want this wall built. No good idea ever goes unchallenged. If there were not some opposition to this one, I would be worried. But when we find out who it is and stop him, or them, then everyone else will fall into line. Even the king will see that we are serious about protecting our people and that we will not be easily dissuaded. He'll be more likely to send pots of gold to get the job done.

"Worry not, Sharzen," he went on, intentionally leaving off the governor's title to demonstrate how little respect he had for it. "This is working out exactly as we want it to."

AFTER THAT FIRST killing, Kral left the settlers alone for a night. He knew their immediate response would be to increase the guards on the wall. He wanted to let those guards be on full alert for one night. When nothing happened, they would relax a little the next one.

The following night, he mixed some more calera root powder. After painting himself again, he swam across a Black River silvered by a crescent moon. When he reached the wall, he couldn't help but be impressed by the progress the builders had made in two days. They must have had every able-bodied man in Koronaka working on the thing, Kral surmised. The wall snaked along between stands of trees, following the flattest line available even when it wasn't the straightest. Where there was a slope, the wall was built at its base so that the defenders on the Aquilonian side would have the advantage of elevation. It looked to be at least eight feet thick, and while Kral wasn't sure if it had reached its final height, in places it towered fifteen feet. Attacking a force secured behind that wall would be a difficult challenge for any Pictish clan.

But Kral wasn't a clan unto himself, though he wasn't far from that. He was a single individual. The bigger the wall grew, the more cover it provided for him.

He had been right in his guess that the Aquilonians would increase the guards. As he walked the tree line observing the heavy stone construction, he noted a number of guards standing or sitting on the wall itself, and heard the voices of others who he couldn't see from his side. There was no way to tell just how many there were from here, without getting up onto the wall.

But he had also had been right that the night with no activity had caused the settlers to let down their guard a bit. He suspected that the night before, all the guards had been on the alert, watching the woods for any sign of an intruder. Tonight, some of them were sitting and chatting, playing with dice, or watching one another instead of the forest. A couple snored loudly at their posts.

Kral smiled. His task would be difficult, but not impossible.

He knew he had to choose his approach carefully, though.

After watching for more than an hour, he was ready to move. Even during that time, the guards had been paying less and less attention to their duties. Many yawned, or sat down to get the weight of armor and weaponry off their feet. The dice games got less serious as the night wore on. Kral wondered if these same guards had been assigned to construction duty during the day. It would account for their exhaustion.

He waited for a thin cloud to move across the sliver of moon that shone, and when it did, he dashed noiselessly over to the base of the wall at one of its highest points. The nearest guard was a dozen feet away and had settled down on his back, with his feet up and his round helmet under his head. He gazed off down the wall toward distant Koronaka and one of the dice games that still continued. On the other side, at twice that distance, a guard sat on the wall's edge with his feet dangling down onto the Aquilonian side, talking to a comrade below.

Kral put his hands against the wall. It was solid. Pushing it down once it had been built to such a height would be no easy task. If he was going to continue to hamper the wall's progress, he'd have to be diligent about attacking it every night.

But that was not his real goal, only an added benefit. He didn't want the wall to be finished because it would make it that much harder for the Picts to drive the settlers out of the region altogether. For now, however, he wanted the Teeth, and he wanted revenge. Slowing the wall's construction was secondary.

The stones were uneven, offering plenty of good hand- and footholds for climbing. Anyway, Kral was a Pict, born in the forests, used to climbing trees and rocks almost before he could walk. Scrambling his way to the top, he waited there in the wall's own shadow for a moment, watching. The nearer guard's breathing was starting to slow—he was already drifting off to sleep. The farther one continued talking about women he had known at home in Numalia. Kral grew bored just listening to him for a minute, and couldn't imagine how his friend could stand to hear him natter on.

Cautiously, Kral lifted his head over the top edge of the wall and turned it in every direction, looking to see if he was observed. So far, he was not. Satisfied, he drew himself higher, the muscles in his upper arms and chest straining to keep his ascent steady and smooth. Once he had brought himself waist high on the wall he rolled over onto it, bringing his legs up, and flattened himself there.

From here, Kral could see more of what transpired on the other side, though if anyone was right at the base of the wall, he couldn't make them out without risking being spotted himself. But he could see small clutches of guards huddled together for companionship, and a few who seemed to take their responsibility seriously walking the lower sections of the wall that hadn't been built up yet.

Until the Aquilonians settled into routines, it would be hard for him to make much progress, he decided. Things were too chaotic, too unpredictable. He couldn't get much accomplished tonight without running the risk of being caught, and there were so many soldiers on duty that he'd have a hard time escaping.

But that didn't mean he was helpless.

He decided to focus on the nearest guard, who by the sound of his breathing had slipped into a gentle slumber.

A pouch dangled from Kral's girdle. From it, he drew two objects he had decided to bring after the first killing— a fist-sized stone and a length of stout leather cord. Remaining as flat as he could, and silently thanking the settlers for making the wall so wide, he moved closer to the snoozing soldier. When he judged himself close enough, he hurled the stone far away, on the Aquilonian side of the wall.

As soon as it hit the ground with a thud, guards reacted, rushing toward the spot and drawing weapons. The guards were noisier than the stone had been. The drumming of their feet and the clink and scrape of blades leaving scabbards and armor jostling drowned out the sounds of Kral's next action.

The ruckus woke the lightly sleeping soldier, but Kral was already on him. He looped the length of cord around the man's throat and yanked it tight, then twisted. The soldier naturally turned himself in the direction that Kral was twisting, trying to ease the pressure on his throat. His hands went to the cord but it bit into his flesh, too tightly for him to get his fingers underneath it. Turning his body was just what Kral had wanted him to do, rendering the guard off-balance and leaning toward the Pictish side of the wall. Kral risked rising to a wide-footed squat and tugged the soldier even more, finally pulling him off the side of the wall.

Kral dropped gracefully to the dirt at the wall's base, landing right next to the soldier, who'd had the wind knocked out of him by his fall. The loop was still around the soldier's neck, though the drop had loosened it. Before the man could recover, Kral grabbed it again and tugged it tight. The man gasped once, then made a gurgling noise as his air was cut off. He tried to buck and fight, but Kral kept the pressure on. In another few moments the man went limp.

The hardest part came next. Kral couldn't let the man just lie there at the wall's base. Soon enough, someone would notice that he was gone. But the soldier was wearing a mail shirt under a leather cuirass, with a reinforced leather skirt and boots, and he was not a small man to begin with.

Kral slipped his arms underneath the soldier's and, straining under the weight, succeeded in lifting his upper torso off the ground. He could drag the man this way, but doing so might still be dangerous. If the soldiers came over the wall with torches, they would surely see the drag marks. Instead, he hunched over and hoisted the heavy burden onto his right shoulder, then forced himself upright, staggering under the load. Breathing heavily, he managed to move one foot, then the other, carrying the unconscious soldier beyond the tree line.

Finally screened from anyone on the wall, he lowered the deadweight to the ground and began to drag him through the thick grass and underbrush. The man's mail jingled faintly, but Kral could still hear shouts, and the commotion on the other side of the wall, he figured, drowned out any sounds he was making.

The farther he got from the wall, the quicker he moved. After a few minutes, it sounded like the soldier was beginning to come around, so Kral positioned his back up against a tree and added a second length of leather cord to the one still wrapped about the man's throat. This, he tied around the tree, leaving it just loose enough that the soldier would be able to breathe. Then he drew his dagger, rested its tip against the man's neck just under the cord, and waited.

Shortly, the man choked and opened his eyes. Kral was right there, pressing the dagger's point into the soft flesh of his neck. "Do not move," he warned the soldier. "You will only hurt yourself. And stay quiet or die."

The soldier's eyes widened, but he seemed to understand Kral's warning. Instead of fighting back or trying to run, he sat still, glaring defiantly into the Pict's eyes.

"What do you want?" he demanded.

"Your soldiers raided the Bear Clan village," Kral answered. "You killed many. Also, you took something that is precious to the Picts but meaningless to you. I must know who took it and where it is."

The soldier tried to shake his head, but the pressure of Kral's dagger dissuaded him. Kral could see the fear in his eyes as he knew he could die at any moment. "I know nothing of what you speak," he said, his voice raspy from the pressure of the cord. "Some of us took spoils of war—weapons, jewelry, and the like. Nothing else that I saw."

"You saw no crown?"

"Crown?" the man echoed. "Of course not."

The man sounded to Kral like he was telling the truth. Kral couldn't be sure. The man's eyes were already bulging and wild with fear. Kral's familiarity with the Aquilonian tongue was not sufficient for him to detect a good liar. But the soldier was afraid for his life, and he hadn't stopped to consider his answer, instead blurting it out as if it was obvious.

"Think about it," Kral urged him. The soldier stared at him as if Kral was a crazy person. Perhaps he was, at that moment.

"I saw no crown," the soldier insisted.

"Very well," Kral replied. Part of him wanted to let the soldier live. He had told Kral what seemed to be the truth and had cooperated with Kral's every demand.

But he knew that the man would go back and tell his fellows that Kral was a single Pict, and a young one at that. The next person Kral tried to question would know that he had let the last one live. It would be harder to get information next time.

But if they were afraid of him, afraid for their lives, then it would get easier and easier.

"I wish you could tell your friends you met me," Kral whispered, "and survived. But you won't be able to do that."

So saying, he poured a handful of powdered calera root from a tiny woven bag and blew it into the man's face. Reflexively, the soldier inhaled it, and he began to kick and yank at the leather thongs that held him.

Kral turned away in shame at what he had done. The man was an enemy, but he had been tied to a tree, not a threat at all, not a participant in a battle. Slaying one's foes in battle was honorable, but killing the helpless was less so.

Kral could only justify it by reminding himself of the broader scale of his mission. He needed revenge for his clan, his family. And more immediately, he needed to find the Teeth of the Ice Bear. Making the fort fear him was the best way to do that.

When the soldier's head slumped forward onto his chest, Kral slipped into the shadows and away from him. As he moved hurriedly through the trees, he could hear an alarm raised from the direction of the wall. The guards had finally realized that one of their number was missing.

By then, Kral was halfway to the Black River, and safety. He hadn't learned anything from the soldier.

But he had learned more about the Aquilonians' intentions, the construction of the wall, the habits of the guards . . . all things that would serve him well, the next time.

And the next.

And again, and again.

As long as it took.

13

THERE WERE OTHER families in Koronaka with girls around Alanya's age, but she had never become close friends with any of them. Partly it was that they were settlers' children, rough-edged, unsophisticated. She felt like they looked down on her for her city ways, even as she considered theirs rude and lacking in the social graces she had learned at home.

But now that the wide world outside Koronaka's walls was closed to her, at least for the time being, she realized that she was going to have to reconsider her choices. She was close to Donial, most of the time, though they were siblings and as such had the same kind of arguments that she was pretty sure brothers and sisters always had. She couldn't just talk to Donial, however. She would go crazy without someone else in her life. She really missed the friends she had back home, with whom she could talk about anything. She had thought she'd found that again, with Kral. But now he was gone, and he was one of the main things she wanted to talk about.

So she started looking about, subtly, for someone in town who she could approach. There weren't many opportunities just to walk up to one and start talking. For the most part, the girls around her age didn't have the kind of leisure time she did, but worked in the fields, or gathered fruits and berries in the forest from which she was now banned, or did laundry, cleaned, ran shops, or the like. And anyway, by now she had been here so long—and admittedly had been generally cool to most of them—that it seemed all the girls already had opinions of her that weren't likely to change easily. She noticed a lot of the townspeople staring at her, lately, talking about her and Donial. Being the daughter of Invictus—and the girl who had consorted with a Pict—had brought her unwelcome attention.

Finally, she identified a girl she thought might be approachable. She worked in her parents' bakery most days. Alanya had had many occasions to go there, fetching bread and biscuits for Lupinius's table and her own father's before he'd gone away. The girl, whose name Alanya had never learned, had always seemed a little shy but not unfriendly.

She went in on this day with a few pieces of silver in her pocket. The shop seemed empty. But after Alanya called out, the girl appeared from a back room. She had a dusting of flour on her cheeks, forehead, and nose, which paled her normally rosy complexion. Her hair was waist length and dark brown, pulled back behind her ears and bound by several leather bands, which Alanya saw because her thick ponytail was draped across her shoulder and had likewise encountered the flour. Alanya burst into laughter at the sight.

The girl wiped her hands on her white apron and smiled. "It got away from me," she said. "The flour."

"I can see that," Alanya replied. "It looks like it got everywhere."

"That happens sometimes," the girl said. "Did you need some bread today?"

Alanya didn't want to conclude her business yet, as that wasn't really why she had come. "What's your name?" she asked. "I'm Alanya."

The girl smiled again. It was a shy smile that took some time to reach its full potential, but when it did Alanya decided it was very endearing. The girl had even, white teeth and full, ruby lips, and if she hadn't been wearing half a bag of flour, she'd have been quite attractive.

"I'm Koniel," she said. "My parents own the shop."

"I guessed that," Alanya said. "My uncle is Lupinius. My father was Invictus, ambassador from Tarantia, but he was killed in the attack on the Pictish village."

The smile faded from Koniel's face, and her lids lowered over her emerald eyes. "I heard about that," she said. "I heard that he died valiantly."

"So they tell me," Alanya replied. "I would rather still have a live father than a dead hero."

"I'm sure that is true," Koniel said. She sounded almost as sorrowful as if it had been her own father.

"It's lonely without him," Alanya said. "I have my little brother, but he—do you have any brothers?"

"One, but he's older. He's in Brythunia."

"So you don't know how annoying a little brother can be. Anyway, it's just us now, with Uncle Lupinius. He is off supervising the building of that silly wall every day. And . . ." She paused and regarded Koniel's face. The girl still looked interested in what she was saying, which was good. "Listen to me, going on like this. I'm sure you have much more important things to do."

Koniel glanced back toward the room she had come from. "I do have some loaves that should go into the oven," she said. "But there is no one else here. Do you want to come back and talk for a while?"

Which was just the invitation Alanya had been hoping for. Making new friends wasn't easy—but neither was it as difficult as she had expected.

• • •

DONIAL HAD ALWAYS enjoyed Koronaka more than his sister had. He liked listening to the stories and rough jokes the woodsmen told, liked seeing the arms and equipment of the soldiers and being allowed to spend time with his uncle's Rangers. His father had arranged for a tutor to keep him and Alanya current on their studies—of Aquilonian language and history, of mathematics and science, and so on. But the Rangers also schooled him in other things. They were teaching him how to use a sword—to date, he favored the short swords of the Aquilonian regulars rather than the longer, heavier weapons some of the Rangers used, which he could lift but not manipulate as well. A couple of the Bossonians had taken it upon themselves to teach him archery, and he practiced on their range twice a week. Other Rangers taught him hand-to-hand combat: wrestling, boxing, close-in knife-fighting. None of these skills would have been taught him back in Tarantia, at least not for a couple more years.

So he liked life on the border. He fit in, better than his older sister, with the local boys. He was rarely bored, and he had made several friends.

He had found one other pursuit that he enjoyed, though this discovery was much more recent. Because of his speed, his agility, and his relatively small frame, he was good at surreptitious behavior. He had followed Alanya into the woods completely undetected. Obviously the upshot of his action had been a tragic one—the death of his own father. He felt terrible about that and could not shake the horrible certainty of his own guilt. He had barely slept since it had happened and could eat only a few bites at a time before the nausea rose in him.

But he didn't object to the soldiers' incursion into Pictish territory during which it had happened. And on its own merits, the surveillance itself, which had involved skills of stealth, silence, tracking, woodcraft, observation, and others, had been fun, though the results were awful.

During his free time, then, he worked on those skills, and practiced following people about the town. He followed Lupinius to Governor Sharzen's office, then trailed the two of them to the fort's gate. They passed through, presumably to oversee work on the wall. He followed Alanya several times, although for the most part she didn't go anywhere or do anything interesting. She seemed to be depressed, moping about their uncle's residence or wandering aimlessly around the town.

Today he tracked her to a baker's shop in town. She entered and stayed inside for a surprisingly long time. Donial had expected her to reappear shortly carrying a basket of breads, but instead he waited and waited. There was no sign that she was ever emerging. Curious, Donial risked moving in closer. The street was relatively clear, since most residents who could carry a stone had been put to work on the wall now that the mass funeral was over. Just the same, Donial checked in both directions before leaving his cover in a sheltered doorway. He dashed at an angle across the road.

His trajectory took him right past the open doorway of the baker's shop. Had anyone been standing inside looking out the door, he'd have been visible for a fraction of a second. But as he passed, he glanced inside and saw no one. He flattened himself against the wall, listening for a moment, then darted around the corner of the building, into an alley where he was beyond the view of anyone looking down the street.

An open window halfway along rewarded his efforts. He approached it silently and squatted beside it, listening. From inside, he heard two female voices engaged in conversation, one of which was definitely Alanya's. ". . . doesn't mean that they're not our enemies," she was saying. "Just that some of them might not be as bad as everyone says."

"Don't let my father hear you saying that," the other voice rejoined. "He believes that every single one of them is a bloodthirsty killer who eats human flesh and bathes in blood."

Alanya laughed. "Seriously?"

"To hear him tell it," the other voice said.

"I can swear to you that isn't the case."

The other girl sounded surprised. "You almost sound as if you know some."

Alanya hesitated. "Will you promise me secrecy?" she asked.

"Of course, Alanya."

"I do." Alanya spoke the two words with enthusiastic certainty. "Or I did, at any rate. He is certainly killed now, in the raid."

"You . . . how did you meet him?" The other girl's voice had gone from surprised to stunned, almost breathless. Donial had heard Alanya's explanation before, and when she started in on it, he wandered away, not wanting to listen to it all again.

What worried him was that now she was telling someone who wasn't family. Telling him, and even Uncle Lupinius and their father, was one thing. But telling outsiders—especially people like this girl, who it sounded like she didn't really know that well—could be dangerous.

The people of Koronaka considered the Picts the enemy—they had been the enemy for a long time. Most were happy about the slaughter at the Bear Clan village and supported the construction of the wall. For Alanya to go around telling people that she had been friendly with one of the Picts could only be a bad idea.

But could he warn her about it? To do so he'd have to admit that he'd been following her again. He wasn't sure how she'd take that news, but he had a feeling she wouldn't be happy about it.

• • •

LUPINIUS AND SHARZEN made their daily inspection
tour of the wall, accompanied on this occasion by Calvert
and a dozen Rangers. Rossun met them near the scene of
the previous night's abduction.

"It's a ghost," he swore. "Or some such being." He spoke
directly to Lupinius, virtually ignoring the governor. "The
other night, when I was on duty, I saw no one, heard nothing.
But someone killed Kelan, practically right under my nose.
I've talked to all the guards who were here last night, and not
a one of them saw any sign of anything wrong. They heard a
noise, they investigated, and found nothing. But when they
returned to the wall—and mind you, Lupinius, they had not
all left the wall, by any means—Franto was gone. Just van-
ished.

"Finally, they found him, tied to a tree, dead. None could
say how he came to be there. Some flattened brush showed
that he could have been dragged part of the way, but not the
entire distance. Otherwise, there were no tracks, coming or
going."

Lupinius nodded, watching Sharzen's reaction to the
tale. The governor's blunt features showed little emotion,
but his eyes roved constantly, flashing from side to side, as
if worried that they would be attacked at any moment. His
massive fists were clenched. Whoever this "ghost" was, he
had Sharzen spooked.

"It is no ghost," Lupinius insisted, aware that Rossun
was using the same description he himself had applied a
couple of days before. "It is a man, and a man can be
caught. A Pict can move through the forest like a spirit."

"I believe you," Rossun said, lowering his voice. "But
some of the men are no longer convinced. Especially the
ones who were here last night and saw the body of their
friend lashed to a tree."

"Convince them," Lupinius ordered.

"I will try," Rossun promised. "The other men would like to hear it from you or the governor," he added. "Coming from me it will not carry as much weight."

"Show us where the body was found," Sharzen commanded him.

"Very well," Rossun agreed. "We will have to go around the wall."

They started walking toward the wall's end. Progress had been made. Even today, after the horrors of the night before, more length was being added. What they needed to do, Lupinius realized, was to build in gates every mile or two. A patrol chased back to the wall by a Pictish force would need to be able to gain access swiftly. And if the soldiers on the inside saw Picts on the other, they needed to be able to get out before the Picts could get away.

Gates would require more soldiers, though. Many more. Every gate would need to be guarded, every hour of the day and night. And once the wall stretched all the way across the border, those guards wouldn't be able to be housed in the existing forts. New barracks would be needed, one near every gate. They would need supplies, roads. They weren't just building a wall, they were building a civilization, here at the edge of the wilderness.

As they walked, he was impressed with the enormity of the task he had set for himself. He had not fully considered all the ramifications of it before, only thought about the potential profit and acclaim that would come his way if it worked. Now he realized it was on a much larger scale than that. If successful—if the king came through with the financing Sharzen had requested—he would not only be wealthy, but he would have reshaped the known world according to his own ideas.

Finally, they had reached the end of the existing construction and passed beyond it and into the forest. Calvert and the Rangers swept ahead, swords at the ready, with Rossun leading them to the spot. Behind them came

Lupinius and Sharzen, along with Traug, a huge, burly Tauran whom Lupinius had put in charge of the construction teams. Traug rarely spoke, except when asked a direct question. Even then his answers rarely exceeded a word or two.

But today, as they walked through the dark, shadowed woods toward the murder site, Lupinius heard his deep, throaty voice behind them. "Don't like this," he said.

"You don't like what?" Sharzen asked him.

Lupinius glanced at the big man. His brown hair was cropped short, making his rounded boulder of a head look even bigger than it might have. He had no visible neck, and his head seemed to sit directly on his enormously muscular frame. His arms were long, but his legs short for his height, so that he seemed almost apelike. He was no coward, but preferred physical labor to battle. Nonetheless, Lupinius was surprised at his response to the governor's query.

"Ghosts," he said simply.

"There are no ghosts here," Lupinius repeated.

"You say so," Traug answered. "Haven't been here at night. We killed many Picts the other day. They may be restless."

It was quite possibly the longest string of sentences Lupinius had ever heard him utter. Before he had a chance to say so, however, they caught up to Rossun and the other Rangers.

"Here is where they found Franto," Rossun said. He was pointing at the trunk of an old oak. A leather cord still bit into its bark, a couple of feet off the ground. Blood had pooled on the dirt and discolored it. "He was sitting against the trunk with that cord around his neck."

Lupinius leaned in and looked at the trunk and the bit of leather hanging there, as if it could tell him anything at all. It couldn't, of course. Apparently only Franto could, and he was dead.

Franto, and this "ghost."

Whoever he was.

Rising and stepping away from the tree, Lupinius caught a glimpse of Sharzen. The fear was even more obvious on him now. Sweat ran in rivulets down his broad cheeks and beaded on his upper lip, which trembled slightly as he regarded the death tree.

"Don't like this," Traug said again.

"Neither do I," agreed the governor.

Lupinius kept quiet. But inwardly, he had to admit that he didn't like it either.

14

SURPRISINGLY, KILLING GOT easier the more Kral did it.

After pulling the man from the wall and killing him in the woods, he gave the settlers a few days to lick their wounds. Either they would drive themselves mad worrying about when he would turn up next, or they would relax again. Kral didn't care which. Both would further his ends.

But he was constantly aware that the Teeth was missing from its proper place in the cave. The longer it was gone, the greater the chance that something horrible would happen—although he still didn't know what that something might be.

So the fourth night found him painted blue, armed with a bow and a knife, and crossing back over the Black. The moon was fuller now, and cast a bright glow on the forested hills leading toward the fort. He had suspected that the Aquilonians might have thought to put guards in the woods approaching the wall by now. But in spite of his cautious approach, he saw none. If they had been there, he would have known it.

When he reached a point from which he could view the wall, he saw that there was a new addition to the construction plan. There was a wooden gateway in place, with double gates about twelve feet across, with the same fifteen-foot height as the walls. Torches burned brightly in sconces mounted on the wall on either side of it. Two helmeted, mail-clad guards stood in front of the gate, looking off toward the woods. If Kral had been less skilled, they could have seen him where he stood.

But he was a Pict, and virtually invisible among his native trees.

The wall's progress these last few days had been impressive. It was beginning to look like a formidable structure. Kral had no idea if the project was confined to this region, or if other settlements along the border were also building walls of their own. If they were, then before too long they could have the Picts completely sealed off from the rest of the world, except by sea. Picts preferred to travel overland whenever possible—they had never made the best seafarers and only took to the water for short journeys or fishing expeditions. They rarely ventured out of their own territory anyway, except on raiding parties, because the civilized world held little appeal to them. But they liked the freedom to come and go as they pleased. Aquilonian advancement into the Westermarck had limited that; a wall across the entire border would end it altogether.

Which meant that he had a third goal. He was already trying to slow building on the wall, but primarily as a means of harassing and disturbing the settlers. Now slowing them down took on greater importance, though still not as critical as finding the Teeth. The trouble was, the bigger the wall grew, the harder it would be for him to have any impact on it. He couldn't single-handedly knock over an eight-foot-thick, fifteen-foot-high section of it.

Still, he reasoned, if he could make them too afraid to be out here working on it, or guarding it, that might ultimately have the same effect. He wondered if he could risk coming here in the daytime to interfere with the building crews.

That, he decided, was for another time. For now he needed to pay attention to his immediate goal—finding out more about where the Teeth had gone. He moved soundlessly up and down the length of the wall, looking for weak points. Finally, he came back to the gate and the two guards who stood there. The wooden gate gave him two ideas.

But two guards . . .

Slipping off the bow that he had carried slung across his back, he fitted an arrow to the string. He was back in more or less the same position he had been when he'd first spotted the gate, just across from it at the tree line. Barely thirty feet separated him from the two guards. He would have to be fast. And accurate.

Arrow for the first one, but what about the second? After considering for a moment, he removed his loincloth and put a rock into it, just about the size of both his fists together. He gave it a couple of practice spins and knew it would work as a makeshift sling.

Satisfied, he aimed the arrow at the guard on the left, and drew back the string. The guard's helmet had no noseguard, so he aimed right between the man's eyes and released the shaft. It flew straight and true, covering the short distance quickly with only the soft rush of wind. Kral saw the point drive into the soldier's face at almost the same moment the soldier finally spotted it coming. He had no time to duck or call out before it hit him, knocking him back into the wooden gate.

Even before the arrow had found its mark, Kral had dropped the bow and retrieved the sling, the ends of which he had tucked into his girdle. The second soldier was just realizing that *something* had happened to his companion when Kral swung the sling in a whistling circle and released one end. The stone sailed across the gap and slammed into the helmet of the second guard. The man buckled against the wooden gate and stumbled over the still form of his comrade. He wasn't unconscious, Kral could tell, just disoriented.

Kral wasted no time.

BY THE TIME Rossun had begun to regain his senses after the blow to his head, there was a naked Pict running across the empty space between the trees and the wall. Rossun shook his head, trying to clear it. The hit had left him dizzy and shaken. He braced his back against the gate and looked up, ready to sound an alarm, only to see that the Pict was airborne. One bare foot, hard as slate, plowed into Rossun's head, smashing it back into the gate again. Rossun saw a bright flash of light, then nothing at all.

Sometime later, he drifted into consciousness again, as if floating up from the bottom of a deep, dark pool. His stomach churned with nausea. When he opened his eyes he felt as if someone were driving steel spikes into his temples. He was sitting down, someplace dark. He tried to stand, but discovered that his hands were tied behind his back. He was lashed to something that he was pretty sure—considering how they had found Franto's corpse—was a tree. The foul taste in his mouth was courtesy of a rag or animal skin that had been stuffed into it, tied down with something else. His helmet was gone, his cuirass unlaced, but he still had the protection of the mail shirt beneath it.

And he was alone. The Pict, if he had really seen what he'd thought, was nowhere to be seen. Rossun tried to spit the cloth from his mouth so he could shout, but it wouldn't budge. Swallowing the wave of agony it caused, he yanked at his arms, trying to break the bonds that held him.

No luck. The Pict had bound him tight.

At least now he knew for certain that it was a man and not a ghost attacking those on the wall.

He continued to struggle, hoping to free himself before the Pict returned. Who knew what he might be up to while Rossun sat here, helpless?

Before long, however, a parting of leaves revealed the tall young Pict—broad-shouldered and well muscled, now wearing a loincloth that he hadn't had before. At his waist hung a long knife. His skin had been painted a dappled blue that made him almost invisible in the moonlight, and dirt was smeared on his arms, legs, and chest—dirt, and maybe blood. In the dim light of the shadowed grove Rossun couldn't tell for sure. His hair was loose and shaggy, his eyes seemingly marked by what looked like a deep, abiding sadness, but Rossun couldn't deny that his features were handsome enough, for a savage.

The young man squatted on the ground near Rossun and lifted something that the Ranger realized was his own broadsword. He held the sword's point toward Rossun's chest. "Sorry to have left you alone," the Pict said. Rossun had no trouble understanding his Aquilonian. "I had other business. But now I would like to talk with you for a brief time."

Rossun couldn't answer, could only glare at his captor and make a muffled, deep-throated growl.

"If I take off the gag, will you swear to remain silent?" the Pict asked him.

Rossun had no choice but to agree. If he didn't, the man would just leave the gag there. At least with it off, he would have some hope of alerting his fellows before the Pict could kill him. He nodded affirmatively.

His captor turned the sword away from him and leaned in just long enough to loosen the strip that held Rossun's gag in place. When it was gone, Rossun was able to shove the ball of skin out of his mouth with his tongue. If his hands had been free, he'd have killed the Pict on the spot for that. As it was, the best he could do was to spit at the young man.

The Pict just laughed and lifted the sword again. "Do you feel better?"

"Untie me, and I will show you how much better," Rossun threatened.

The Pict laughed again. "I will untie you when you have told me what I want to know."

"Then you might as well kill me now."

The Pict's smile faded. "You know not what I want."

"It matters not," Rossun assured him. "I will tell you nothing."

"Loyalty is a good thing," the Pict acknowledged. "But loyalty to the wrong purpose is not."

"Who's to say what purpose is right or wrong?" Rossun returned.

"Not I," the Pict replied. "But my heart tells me that the slaughter of a people with whom you had a truce is no noble purpose."

Rossun had no argument to make against that. He considered shouting once again, but knew the Pict would run the blade through him if he tried. Better to keep the youth talking, to see if an opportunity for escape presented itself. "You may be right," he admitted. "I do not pretend to know the reasons for the things our leaders do. I go where I'm sent and fight who I'm told. Are you of the Bear Clan?"

"I am," the Pict told him.

"And you survived the battle?"

"I was not in the village when it was attacked," the young man said.

Rossun nodded, things becoming clearer to him now. This young Pict had been away, and came home to find his people obliterated, his home in ruins. No wonder he was angry. No wonder that indelible sadness had taken root in his eyes.

On the other hand, he had killed Kelan, and Franto, and delayed work on the wall for days. He was no wronged innocent but, young as he was, rather a hardened warrior who thought nothing of taking Aquilonian lives. Rossun just had to steel himself against the Pict's tales of woe.

"Truce or no truce, our peoples are at war," Rossun said.

"I agree."

"Then why do you think I—"

The youth interrupted him. "What I seek has nothing to do with the war between Pict and Aquilonian, nothing to do with Aquilonians at all," he explained. "It is sacred to the Picts, without value to anyone else. It was stolen from our village, during the raid."

"Spoils of war—" Rossun began, but again the young man cut him off.

"Not of war," he said. "This is not a weapon, not even treasure. It is of holy significance only. As I said, there is no value in it to Aquilonians, or any other people."

"And I should believe this just because you tell it to me?"

"If you had seen it, you would know," the Pict said. "You could see for yourself that it is not jewel-encrusted, not precious in that way."

"What is this object?" Rossun asked. He couldn't think of anything that he had seen taken away from the village that might fit the man's description.

"We call it the Teeth of the Ice Bear," the Pict replied. "It is a crown, made of bone, decorated with bear's teeth."

"The crown?" Rossun asked without thinking. He had not, in fact, seen it. But he had heard someone say that Lupinius had something like that. It sounded like a trifle, something he had only picked up as a curiosity. The soldier who had mentioned it said that Lupinius had laughed at himself for even bothering to carry it back to Koronaka.

"Then you *have* seen it," the Pict said anxiously. New enthusiasm flashed in his dark eyes.

"I have not," Rossun corrected. What harm, though, in letting this young savage know that he knew where it might be found? If Lupinius really didn't care about it, perhaps he would give it up. If that would satisfy the Pict, make him go away and stop attacking the wall, wouldn't it be worth it? "But I know who has it."

"Who?" the Pict demanded angrily.

"His name is Lup—never mind that," Rossun said. "The point is, I believe that I can retrieve it for you. We want peace with you. You have killed enough of us already. If you promise to leave us alone, I can get you that crown."

The Pict looked like he was considering Rossun's offer. "If I knew that I could trust you . . ."

"Why do you think you cannot?" Rossun wanted to know.

"As soon as I released you, you could run back behind the protection of the fort," the youth said. "Raise a war party and return to the Bear Clan village to finish your job, now that you know I yet live."

"I would not," Rossun tried to assure him.

The Pict looked sad as he lifted Rossun's big sword again. "No, you will not."

The young Pict tossed his weapon aside, drew some powdered substance from a pouch at his belt, and hurled it at him like he was tossing a cloud. Rossun blinked, inhaled, and his senses seemed to shut down. A paroxysm of coughing took him, then he knew no more.

15

GOVERNOR SHARZEN KNEW he was at a crossroads. He also knew that he had ceded control of his own future long ago. He wasn't even the one who would decide which road he would take. At Lupinius's urging, he had invested so much of his own political future in the wall that if anything happened to the project he wasn't sure how he would recover. Unfortunately, although progress was being made, there were still major problems to contend with. Another two bodies had turned up this morning, one soldier and one of Lupinius's Rangers, who had, like Franto, been taken away from his post and killed. To make things worse, the ghost had used the guards' own torches to set the soldier's body on fire, and the wooden gate structure as well.

To make things worse, Traug, the construction supervisor, had just left his office. He had, in his own almost monosyllabic fashion, reported talk of mutiny. He told Sharzen that many of the workers, particularly the ones who were not also soldiers and just doing the job for the few coins promised them, were thinking about not coming

back to work because of the ghost's activities. That was
how they were referring to the interloper, just about everyone calling him—or them—the Ghost of the Wall. The
name had stuck. That, as much as anything else, was a sign
of how much impact his nocturnal raids had made on
morale.

Maybe if Sharzen had been stronger—mentally, not
physically, as there were few who could match him for
sheer brute muscle—he wouldn't have let Lupinius twist
him around until he was essentially doing the other man's
bidding. He was, after all, the governor of the province,
and therefore supposed to be the man in charge. But he had
fallen under Lupinius's sway, and now the man walked all
over him, virtually ordering him around as if he were some
kind of servant. And there was little Sharzen could do
about it, at this point. Lupinius could easily expose him for
the puppet he had been on so many occasions.

He needed to decide what to do about the wall and how
to stem the workers' complaints. Or else he needed to force
Lupinius to figure out what to do.

He sipped sour wine from a heavy brown ceramic mug,
winced at the taste, and took a larger swallow. There was a
whole barrel of the stuff in his pantry. It didn't taste good,
but it was strong. Maybe seeking oblivion in that was his
best bet. He could forget about his problems, if only for
a brief time.

He was raising the mug again when he heard the pound-
ing of hoofbeats outside, then the clatter of someone rushing up the stairs and drumming on the front door. Muffled
voices, his serving staff letting the rider in. A moment later
the aged, bald Quelo opened the door to his office and
stared at the floor. "Malthus, back from Tarantia," he announced.

Sharzen swallowed hard. He hadn't expected Malthus
to return for several days, at the earliest. The man had been
sent with a message for King Conan, about the death of his

ambassador, the breaking of the truce, and the wall project. Sharzen's message had blamed the Picts for all three. He had told Malthus to wait for a response. The man must have exhausted half a dozen horses to have gone all the way there and returned so quickly.

Malthus was red-faced and haggard, as if he had ridden day and night without stopping. He stopped just inside the door, out of breath. He still wore a cloak, riding breeches, and boots.

"Did you see the king?" Sharzen asked without prelude.

Malthus took a deep breath and nodded, his long, dark hair, wet with sweat, shaking as he did. "Aye," he reported. "I saw him."

"And?"

"And he gave me this," Malthus replied, drawing a scroll from beneath his cloak.

"Well, don't just stand there!" Sharzen exclaimed, extending a hand for the scroll. Malthus moved forward and put it in Sharzen's open hand, and Sharzen unrolled it. The words on it were written in a steady hand.

Sharzen's hands were considerably less steady as he read them. By the time they reached the bottom, he was shaking so much he could barely hold on to it.

ALANYA WALKED HOME carrying a basket of fruits that she'd had to buy since she was no longer allowed to go beyond the walls to pick her own. The town had been usually quiet recently, and today was no exception. Her own footsteps sounded loud on the cobblestone streets, and on the ones that were just bare dirt there were precious few other footprints around to cover hers. She could see the path that she had taken on her way out.

But up ahead, she saw a couple of young women, maybe her age or a little older, wearing the raw, simple clothing the settlers favored. She'd had several conversations with

Koniel over the last few days, and had realized just how much she had been missing having a confidante. Now she saw the girls ahead glance back her way. She wondered if maybe there might be opportunity for more friendships there. She quickened her pace a little, affixed a smile to her face.

Instead of waiting for her, or coming her way, however, the girls sped up and hurried around a corner. Surprised, Alanya quickened her own pace. When she reached the corner behind which the girls had disappeared, she looked in that direction. They hadn't gone far, but had met up with another one. They were all looking back toward the corner, gesturing and laughing in that direction. When Alanya came into view, they stopped suddenly and turned away.

Alanya froze in place, instantly heartsick. It was no trick to figure out that they had been talking about her, laughing at her. Before, they would have simply ignored her, or perhaps, because of her father's death, even pitied her. Nothing had changed, that she knew of. Except that she had confided in Koniel.

Which could only mean that Koniel hadn't been as trustworthy as she had thought. Fighting back tears, Alanya headed for home. So far, her record in choosing friends here on the border had been a sorry one—a Pict, her friendship with whom had reignited a dormant war and gotten her father killed, and a local girl who couldn't wait to tell all her real friends about the pathetic city girl who had confided in her.

The urge to run away, simply to flee the place welled up in her, as it did more and more frequently. Koronaka was a stifling prison, no kind of home. Not for her. The road to Tarantia was long and dangerous, with bandits and highwaymen and who knew what other perils along the way.

But would facing those perils—would death itself—be

worse than staying here, where she was so utterly miserable and alone?

More and more, she thought she knew the answer.

KRAL HAD TAKEN to sleeping during the day, usually under the shade of one tree or other. He didn't sleep on the site of his old village, but somewhere down near the base of the hill. He changed spots often in case the Aquilonians sent anyone looking for him. So far he had seen no sign of that.

One day he woke up to the sound of voices speaking Pictish. He moved gracefully and silently between the trees until he came across Klea and Mang. Both looked drawn, weary, as if the journey to other Pict clans had worn heavily upon them. Kral ran to them with open arms, welcoming them back.

A few minutes later they all sat on rocks near the hill's foot. "How went your journey?" Kral asked them.

Mang sucked in a deep breath, then blew it out, a bitter look on his face. "They agree that the loss of the Teeth is a terrible blow," he said. "And they agree that recovering the crown is of vital importance. But they do not agree on how to go about getting it back."

"I have been working on that part," Kral admitted. "But what about the rest? What about uniting, finally, against these invaders?"

Klea picked up the thread. "Each clan says it is willing to unite to drive the settlers from our lands," she announced. "But then, each clan also has specific conditions that must be met, old rivalries that must be acknowledged, and so on. This is why you see us not at the head of an army but rather by ourselves again. We can unite the clans, we believe, but it will take time and effort."

"What of you, Kral?" Mang asked, wiping dust from the road off his face. "How have you occupied yourself? Have you had any success in your search for the Teeth?"

At first, Kral wasn't sure how much to tell them. He had been intentionally vague before they had left. He didn't think they would object to his tactics. They understood that the Aquilonians were the enemy, as surely as he did. But still, he hesitated. His whole plan was built around secrecy, around stealthy attacks, and using the fear of the unknown to gain information. He knew that Klea and Mang would never reveal his identity to the Aquilonians. Nonetheless, he felt strange telling anyone else what he had been doing.

Both stared at him, he realized. Waited for him to answer. Uncomfortable, he picked up a pebble, turned it in his fingers, and hurled it toward the top of the hill. "I believe I am making progress," he said.

"How?" Klea asked. "What kind of progress?"

Kral felt his face flush, surprised at his own embarrassment. "I have been . . . visiting Koronaka. The settlers have been building a wall, which seems intended to keep us on one side and them on the other. I have been doing what I can to disrupt the building of that wall, and at the same time trying to find out who has the Teeth, or where it is."

"Trying to find out . . ." Klea echoed.

"I have been killing them, one by one," Kral announced. "Questioning them to find out what they know, if anything, then leaving them dead for the others to find. Teaching them to fear me."

Klea looked astonished at his revelation, but Mang just nodded with grim satisfaction. "Good," he said. "The more of them dead, the better."

"But have you learned anything this way?" Klea asked.

"I believe so," Kral replied. "I think I have a clue. Tonight, I will follow up on it."

"Perhaps you should wait before going again," Mang suggested. "When the clans have united—"

"It will be too late," Klea interrupted. "You said it yourself, the more dead the better. And if Kral thinks he can find the Teeth this way, he needs to continue on with it."

"It sounds very dangerous," Mang pointed out.

"It is," Kral said. "I'm not afraid of danger."

"A little danger is a small price to pay if he can find the crown," Klea observed.

"I am happy for Kral to kill as many settlers as he can," Mang countered, addressing her as if Kral weren't sitting right there. "But I worry that they will decide to move the crown away from Koronaka if he continues with these raids. If he were to wait until we have a unified force that could invade their fort, with the same fury and overwhelming numbers which with they must have attacked us, then—"

"Then their defensive wall may well be finished," Kral cut in. "I don't know if it's just an effort here at Koronaka, or all across the borderlands. But I fear that it means a greater effort at holding us off, perhaps a return to the days of all-out war. Waiting is no option, Mang. As much as I respect your age and wisdom, I must insist that you let me keep up what I've already begun."

Mang leaned forward, picking up a stick, and began to doodle in the dirt. "My only worry is that you will be killed," Mang said. "Then where will we be? Unless you tell us what you have learned, and how to continue, all your efforts will have been for naught."

"Very well," Kral acknowledged. "Listen, and I will tell you everything . . ."

16

"TELL ME THIS again," Lupinius demanded angrily. He was on his feet, pacing his flagstoned courtyard. Sharzen sat on the steps with the scroll on his lap and a hangdog look on his face. "He refuses us the funds?"

"And insists that we reinstate the truce," Sharzen added. "'I sent an ambassador to the borderlands to cement the peace, not to destroy it,'" he read. "According to Malthus, the king was furious. I'm glad I wasn't there myself. Malthus thinks he was ready to tear someone limb from limb."

"Once a barbarian," Lupinius said. "What do you expect?"

"So, should we abandon the wall?" Sharzen wondered.

Lupinius threw his hands in the air. The governor was so helpless without him. "Of course not! The wall secures the peace. The only way to guarantee peace with savages is to limit contact between them and civilized people. The wall is the best way to accomplish that."

"But . . . without financial help from Tarantia, I don't know how we will be able to afford to continue," Sharzen moaned. "We have already put so much of our treasury into it, counting on reimbursement from the king."

None of Lupinius's private funds had gone into the wall project, and he intended to keep it that way. But he wanted Sharzen to keep the wall going, didn't want him to decide that it had been a bad idea from the start. To admit failure might give Sharzen the idea that he didn't need Lupinius after all.

Anyway, his own financial situation was perilous enough as it was. He had to pay a household staff, plus all his Rangers. He had been counting on some treasure from that Pictish hoard, then come out of it with nothing but a stupid crown of bones and teeth. His brother had always been good for emergency loans, but now he was dead. Invictus owned an estate back in Tarantia, but Lupinius had no way to know what that was worth, if anything. It had been years since he had seen it. And now this—a barbarian king who couldn't even see the future when it was handed to him on a platter.

Living like a gentleman out here on the border wasn't nearly as costly as doing so back in the city, but there were still expenses. His head whirled as he tried to figure out his next step. It didn't help that Sharzen slumped on his steps with his eyes liquid, looking like a whipped puppy.

"I don't care how you pay for it," Lupinius growled. "Raise taxes if you need to. Financing is your problem, Sharzen. I need to think about how best to continue, and to get the other settlements to join our effort, in the face of this . . . this minor setback."

"Minor?" Sharzen echoed. "Malthus said the king was furious."

"And a thousand miles away!" Lupinius reminded him. "He can't hurt you, Sharzen."

"I serve at his pleasure," Sharzen pointed out. "Need I remind you that Aquilonia appoints the provincial governors? He could recall me in an instant." He shuddered violently.

"Recall me to Tarantia, in fact. Where he *could* reach me. Or just throw me in prison for the rest of my life."

"You overreact dramatically," Lupinius said. He thought the sight of the man's panic would make him physically ill. He turned to gaze at the cloudless indigo sky over the roof of his home. The sun was almost down, streaks of pink shooting into the dark sky. Another night, another opportunity for the Ghost of the Wall to strike. "I think you should go home, Sharzen, and let me think."

"If . . . if that is what you want," Sharzen agreed. "But if you have any ideas, be sure you let me know right away."

"I always have ideas, Sharzen. You should have learned that by now, if nothing else."

"I know," Sharzen said as he rose from the stairs. He rolled the scroll and tucked it away in his robes. "I am only afraid that this time, your ideas may have brought ruin to both of us."

THE GUARDS WERE accustomed to Kral's taking his victims from on top of the wall, or in front of it. Since it was his intention to keep them guessing, never to let them figure out his next move, he decided to do just the opposite.

Tonight, he was going *inside* the wall.

He went to one of his usual spots to examine their defenses. There were two guards stationed together every fifty feet or so, some with dogs on leashes sniffing at the breeze. Torches were mounted on the wall's surface between them, and firepots to illuminate the night on the top above every pair of guards. The gateway Kral had burned had already been rebuilt, and four guards surrounded it.

Getting past a force of that size would be nearly impossible.

On the other hand, they clearly expected him to try anyway. So he would. He would accomplish the impossible, just not the way they thought he would.

He wouldn't go over the wall, after all.

He would go *around* it.

The settlers had been building the wall away from Ko-ronaka as quickly as possible, then once the structural base had been laid, building it up with a combination of stone and logs. But it was still little more than four miles long. Kral melted into the wooded shadows and made his way to the northern end of the wall, then continued for another half mile or so. The guards were posted the length of the wall, but not into the forest beyond that. In the woods, he heard night birds, the strident complaints of crickets, the rustle of small animals. Those creatures didn't even pause in their activities, so silent was the young Pict.

Once he was sure he was well past the end of the wall, he cut to the southeast, taking him onto the Aquilonian side of the wall. Again, he traveled much farther than was absolutely necessary because he wanted to make sure he was past where the guards would be stationed. He traveled quickly, with the easy pace of one raised in the woods.

Still certain that he had been unobserved, Kral turned back to the south, in a direction that would bring him toward Koronaka. Toward the most developed section of the wall. After a short while he could hear noises from the wall—voices, laughter, the sounds of hard-bitten men trying to keep themselves alert through the long, cool night. The trees continued to shield him from view as he approached the wall from the side he had not yet seen. When the flickering of torches and the steady glow of lanterns began to be visible through the foliage, he stopped to survey the scene and figure out a plan of action.

From here, the construction looked very different. The wall was buttressed on the inside by a series of logwork braces. Small timber buildings had been thrown up, as well, particularly in the area of the gates. They looked like small cabins, built up against the wall itself, using that structure as the back wall of each cabin. The roofs of the cabins were flat, and could serve as expanded parapets for soldiers to look out over the top of the wall.

The cabins seemed quiet. Kral suspected that they were barracks, where soldiers could sleep when they weren't on duty. The torches and lanterns were kept away from those, and guards were keeping their distance—so as, Kral guessed, not to awaken those slumbering within.

Both facts told Kral that those cabins were where he wanted to be.

The idea crystallized in his mind as he weaved through the trees toward the nearest of the cabins. He had been trying to create an impression among the settlers of a mysterious force of nature, someone who could attack anytime, anywhere, without warning. The doubling and redoubling of the guards showed that his plan was working, at least on some kind of overall, strategic level.

But what he also wanted was for the average soldier to be personally terrified of him, so that when he did single one out, that soldier would rather tell him what he wanted to know than try to resist.

Instead of trying to pick off alert guards, who were watching one another's backs closely, he would drop in on sleeping soldiers.

The last fifty feet before the door to the barracks was clear ground—some tall grass and a few bushes, but no trees. Kral took the bow from his back and set it beside a tree, then added the quiver of arrows. He would be up close to his enemies tonight. Knife distance. Calera root distance.

He dropped to a crouch before he left the cover of the trees. The moon cast a silvery glow on the grasses, but Kral knew the focus of the guards was toward the other side of the wall, not this side. He dashed to the nearest of the larger bushes. Flattening himself, he crawled through the tall grass, oblivious to the scratching and clawing of thick stalks, rocks, and other objects against his bare, painted flesh.

He didn't try to rush, but made sure that his progress was steady and unobserved. As he got closer to the barracks, he stopped frequently, raising his head to look out and make sure no one's attention was turned toward him.

Finally, he was within a short sprint of the barracks door.

Checking once more to be sure he was clear, he rose for the last dash. Reaching the door, he stopped and pressed his ear against the wood, listening. From within, he could hear only an erratic snoring. No way to tell how many men he would find inside. At least it didn't sound like anyone was awake.

Pushing against the door to keep noise down, he worked the latch and opened the door just enough to slip inside. The interior was dark, but he had been out in the night for long enough that he could see fairly well by the dim light that filtered in through cracks in the hastily built wall and the one small slit of a window. There were six bunks, three occupied at the moment. In one of them, across the room by the window, the snoring man lay on his back with one knee bent, sticking up in the air. Nearer, a slender young man slept on his stomach, one arm hanging off the side of the bed and scraping the floor. In the bunk beside his, a burly, grizzled veteran snoozed with his mouth open.

The rest of the room was open and plain. Weapons ranked against one wall, shelves and hooks for clothing and armor. The soldiers no doubt prepared food and ate by the fire pits outside.

Kral decided to concentrate on the veteran. He would rather have chosen the younger soldier, who was the closest to him. But the veteran would put up a fiercer battle than would the young one, and it was possible that the young one would be terrified into silence if he woke up. The snorer was just too loud, and Kral was afraid that he would make a racket. So he moved quietly through the room, the sound of his passage drowned out by the man's raucous breathing.

Standing at the snorer's side, Kral drew his pouch from his girdle and bent over the man. He reached out and closed the man's nostrils with the fingers of his left hand. The man instantly woke up, eyes wide, gasping for breath. Kral blew a handful of calera root powder into the man's open mouth. With his left hand, he squeezed the man's nose, holding his head still. The man struggled for air, inhaling the powder as he did. He made a soft gagging sound as the powder took effect.

That was enough to alert the old veteran, however. He snapped awake and began to sit up. Kral moved faster. He drew his knife and knelt on the man with one leg. Pressing him back down against his bunk, Kral dug the knife into his neck just enough to make it clear that he could dispatch the man quickly. The younger soldier snoozed on, unaware.

"You have a commander whose name begins with Lup," Kral whispered. "Who is he?"

The soldier's eyes were bright and liquid in the faint light. Kral smiled, satisfied that his reputation had indeed spread before him. "You know who I am, right?" he asked.

The soldier nodded his affirmation.

"Then tell me what I want to know."

The soldier's neck twitched as he swallowed back his fear. "Figure it out for yourself, you son of a misbegotten cur."

Kral increased the pressure of the knife's point and brought his face very near the bearded Aquilonian's. "Last chance," he hissed. "Who is Lup?"

In the next bunk, the young soldier stirred and turned. "Lupinius?" he suggested, still mostly asleep.

"Quiet!" the veteran barked.

Kral knew his control of the older man was slipping by the second. The man reached for his wrists, so Kral shoved down hard on the knife, driving it into the soldier's neck. The powerful man bucked and threw Kral off him. Rolling out of the bunk, he snatched up a sword he had hidden under his blankets.

Kral scrambled to keep his balance on the floor but his legs shot out from beneath him. His knife was gone, jammed into the man's neck but apparently having missed any vital points. The soldier yanked it from his neck, threw it behind him. Blood ran from the wound, but not in the jets that Kral had hoped for.

In the other bunk, the young soldier was coming around, realizing that there was trouble. "Narth?" he asked.

"Go fetch the guard," he said. "Raise an alarm. I think we've caught the Ghost of the Wall."

"You think you can hold me?" Kral asked. "I am a ghost, after all."

"You look human to me," the one called Narth said. "Go, Vincius."

Kral knew that he had only seconds before this turned into a very bad situation indeed. Once Vincius was out that door, he would be surrounded and vastly outnumbered within moments. He should have killed the young one as soon as he had come in instead of counting on fear to paralyze him.

Now he had to stop the man before he opened the door. "Stop, Vincius!" he pleaded. Vincius hesitated as if unsure whether or not to obey.

From atop his bunk, Narth scowled down at Kral with his short sword raised to strike a killing blow. "You're in no position to give orders, little Pict."

"Narth, should I . . . ?" Vincius began.

Narth started to growl an answer, but Kral kicked out with both feet, into the bottom of the bunk on which Narth was still supporting most of his weight. The bunk tipped over and sent Narth sprawling. Vincius stayed where he was, as if rooted to the spot.

Kral leapt up to take instant advantage of Narth's fall. He plowed over the bed and threw himself on Narth, preventing the soldier from reaching the sword he had dropped when he fell. Narth struggled furiously, but he was already weakened from the neck wound and dizzied from the fall. Gripping both of Narth's wrists, Kral bashed him in the jaw with his own forehead. Each blow drove the soldier's head back against the hard-packed dirt floor. Narth grunted with pain, spittle flecked the corners of his mouth. Finally, Kral dared to release one of Narth's arms and grabbed the soldier's wounded neck instead. Narth let out a pained whine, but Kral kept the pressure on until the man lost consciousness.

Instantly, he released Narth and turned his attention to Vincius. The younger soldier still hadn't left the barracks. Instead, he had chosen a pike from the rack of weapons by the door. When Kral turned to face him, Vincius was bearing down on him with the point of the pike. Kral was still straddling Narth's lifeless form.

As Vincius lunged with the long weapon, Kral ducked under it and scooped up Narth's short sword. He brought the sword up in time to block a second thrust. Vincius poked at him a third time. This time Kral turned and let the pike's head slide past him, then grabbed the shaft and yanked on it. As the inexperienced Vincius lost his balance and teetered forward, Kral drove the short sword up and into his breast. Vincius started to scream, but Kral released the pike, rose, and clapped his hand over the man's mouth. He shoved the young soldier down onto the nearest bunk, drew the sword from his chest, and drove it home once more.

Pinned to the bunk, Vincius gurgled his last, wet breath.

Kral listened at the door, this time trying to determine if anyone outside had heard the struggle. There were no immediate sounds of alarm, so he opened the door a crack and looked out.

All was quiet and dark. The guards continued their watches, looking out toward the Black River, no doubt wondering when the ghost would appear.

But he was already inside. And, at last, he knew something he hadn't a few minutes before.

A name.

Lupinius.

17

LUPINIUS COULDN'T SLEEP.

Just a couple of days before, everything had been going so well. Now it had turned bad, all of it. The wall project was doomed, and when Sharzen figured that out it would be the end of Lupinius's control over him. Koronaka would likely be bankrupted by then, or the governor would have raised taxes so high that the citizens would revolt. Either scenario could end with a noose around Lupinius's neck.

Sitting in his office, he touched that neck with his fingers. He liked it the shape it was, not stretched.

Regardless of the wall project, his own fortune was dangerously depleted. Without an influx of some kind, he would have to let the Rangers go, reduce the household staff. He had used his special relationship with Sharzen to avoid paying taxes at all. But if that relationship was threatened, he could be facing serious difficulties there as well. He had hoped the so-called Pictish Hoard would help with that situation, though all it had done was to make him increasingly nervous.

He had stored the ugly thing in a wooden box in his bedroom, but he still knew nothing about it. Every time he dared ask someone with more experience of things Pictish than he had, he was met with blank stares. Worse, he couldn't help believing that with every subtle attempt at gathering information, he was only letting on that he had the thing and believed it to be of some value. Those few Rangers who had seen it had believed it to be simply an object of curiosity. He didn't want it known that magical forces seemed to swirl around it.

He had nearly decided that it was back in Aquilonia, not here on the border, that he would be able to find answers. There, he knew people who studied such things. People who were worldly, educated. The provincials on the border couldn't be trusted.

Leaving Koronaka would mean giving up his home here, his power over Sharzen. But back in Tarantia, his brother's estate sat empty. No matter what condition it had fallen into, it would serve as a place to find shelter while he researched the crown. And if it had been well kept, it would be more than that—perhaps even the foundation a new fortune.

He stood and paced, listening at the open window every now and then, although he didn't know for what. The household was asleep; it seemed the whole town was.

He was about to give up and try going to sleep again—fruitless though he suspected it would be—when he heard the rush of feet slapping the flagstones outside. The last time a rider had come to the house, it had been Sharzen with more bad news. He hoped that wasn't the case with this runner.

Since the staff was already asleep, he went to the door himself. A soldier stood outside, breathing heavily, a sheen of sweat gleaming in the light from the lanterns.

"What is it?" Lupinius wanted to know.

"Sir," the soldier said. He paused to gulp in a huge swallow of air, and continued. "A soldier named Narth has been attacked by the Ghost of the Wall, but lived to tell of it.

Barely, I'm afraid. If he sees the sun rise, I'll be surprised."

Lupinius was rapidly losing patience. "It's late, man. Has this anything to do with me?"

"Yes," the soldier said, his face reddening even more with chagrin than it had with the effort of his run. "This soldier, Narth. He said that when the Ghost attacked—they were sleeping, in their barracks—that another soldier, a young one with little experience or wisdom, accidentally mentioned your name. The Ghost was specifically asking about you, and the other one, Vincius—the Ghost killed him, and one other, as well—revealed your name before he was awake enough to understand what was going on. Narth can barely breathe, is in incredible pain, but he wanted to be sure you were warned. We'll post a guard around your house. Soldiers are on the way now."

"Very well," Lupinius said, his mind already beginning to churn over the possible consequences of this report. He didn't wait for the soldier to answer but simply closed his door.

He had been right, unfortunately. More bad news.

But on top of the rest of it, perhaps news that pushed him over the edge of the decision cliff he had been standing near.

There seemed only one course of action remaining open to him. He just had to be brave enough to take it.

ALANYA THOUGHT SHE heard noises elsewhere in the house, but she was deep in slumber, dreaming that she sat in a golden meadow with her mother and father, eating velvety fruits. Before she could rouse herself enough to investigate she had fallen asleep again. The second time a noise intruded on her rest, however, she snapped awake as suddenly as if sleep was a door that had been thrown open.

Instantly alert, she turned and put her bare feet on the cold stone floor of her room. She sat still for a long while, listening intently. A house had a particular quality of sound, she had often felt, when it was empty, and another sound, almost like deep breathing, when it had people asleep inside.

Just now, though, there was a third sensation, a different quality. Alanya wasn't sure how to interpret it. She couldn't hear anything specific, nothing she could put a name to, anyway. She just felt some indefinable sensation of *difference*.

As quietly as she could, Alanya crossed to her door and eased it open. She stopped just inside, peering into the dark house and listening for anything. For a moment she considered retrieving her shielded lantern from the bureau, but then decided against it. Hearing nothing out of the ordinary, she continued into the hall.

And then she heard it again—a soft, barely perceptible click, as of a door closing.

She froze where she was, trying to ascertain where the sound might have originated. After a few seconds, she heard something else, something that might have been a cautious exhalation. So someone was awake in the quiet house. But who?

Probably Uncle Lupinius, she decided. He hadn't been sleeping well the last several nights. As much as she sometimes disliked him, she didn't wish him any harm. She made her way toward his office to see if he was in there.

But before she reached it, a form came into view in the open doorway, silhouetted against the dark office, black on black. The person's sudden appearance startled her. Her breath caught, and then held, because the person was too short to be Lupinius, too tall for Donial, and too muscular—and nearly naked—for the rest of the staff.

She recognized his build and the general shape before she could make out his features. Even so, her heart leapt as she realized who stood before her.

"Kral!" she said, her voice a loud whisper.

He took a few quick strides toward her, holding his right hand out in a warning gesture. "Quiet, Alanya," he said. "If I am discovered here . . ."

At first, she thought he must have come to find her. She could hardly believe he was alive, much less right in front of her. She closed the rest of the gap and threw her arms around him, drawing him toward her in a furious embrace. "Oh, Kral," she whispered. "I'm so glad you're alive."

"As am I," Kral replied. Even as he spoke, a strong metallic smell reached her, and she drew back.

"Is that . . . Kral, you're covered in blood!"

Kral held her gaze, his eyes glittering darkly in the shadowed space. "I . . . I am not the same person you knew before," he admitted. She saw that he was not only drenched in blood but had painted much of his face and chest with some kind of blue coloring, whether as a war paint or to make him blend into the shadows she had no idea. "I have seen too much, done too much. I should not even be talking to you now."

"What do you mean, Kral?" Alanya wanted to know. "Come, in my room we will have more privacy."

Kral stood his ground. "I have much to do, and it is dangerous for me to be here," he said.

"Dangerous . . . ?" Gradually, like the sun rising at dawn, understanding came to her. Kral, blood-soaked and sneaking through the house in the night. A Pict, avenging his clan. The Ghost of the Wall everyone was talking about. "Kral, are you . . . ?"

He seemed to understand the words she was hesitant to say. Now he did look away from her, as if unable to continue looking into her eyes. "They call me a ghost," he said.

"But . . . why did you come here?"

"I am looking for one called Lupinius," he said. "I was told that this is his house. He is not much loved among the soldiers, else they would have worked harder to hide him from me."

"It is his house," Alanya said, her voice catching with emotion. "He . . . he is my uncle. My brother and I live here, since . . . since my father was killed in the attack on your village."

"As was mine," Kral said quietly.

"Why do you seek him?"

"He took something that belongs to my people," Kral said. Alanya could tell that he was uncomfortable talking here in the open. But he had declined her invitation to go into her room. He wanted to conclude his business and get away, and she was delaying him. From the stories she had heard, she was lucky he hadn't simply killed her as soon as he saw her.

But whatever had happened, whatever he had done, he was still Kral. He would not hurt her, she was certain. "What is it?"

"A crown. Have you seen it? It is made of bones, and huge bear teeth."

She had heard something like that mentioned in passing, since the raid, but had not seen it for herself. "No," she answered. "You did not find it in his office?"

"It is not there," Kral declared.

"His bedroom, then," Alanya suggested. Suddenly realizing what would likely occur if Kral met Lupinius there, her hand shot to her mouth. "But do not—"

"The Teeth is the most sacred object of our people and my responsibility to bring back," Kral told her. "No matter what the price, I must find it."

"But . . . he is my uncle."

Kral's face betrayed no emotion. "Everyone I knew, all of my family, was slaughtered by the raid on my village, Alanya. Your uncle killed a holy man and stole a sacred object. If I need to kill him, I will, but I must have that crown."

Alanya knew that she could not appeal to reason, for his argument was impossible to counter. And she couldn't appeal to emotion because her loss, horrible as it had been, was nothing compared to his.

"Let me look," she suggested. "If he wakes, I can just say I was looking for something else. It will be awkward, but no one has to be hurt."

Kral hesitated, then agreed. He held his hands out, indicating a circle that was about head-sized. "This is how large it is," he said. "Bones and teeth—you cannot mistake it for anything. I'll be listening outside the door. You must search the entire room, and if things turn bad, I will go in. And I will kill him for what he did to my clan."

Alanya felt a chill, as Kral's words sank into her bones. She was the only thing that stood between her uncle—the man as responsible as any, she believed, for the death of her father—and Kral, a Pict, an enemy of her people. Whom she had known for only a matter of days, really.

And yet, if it came to conflict between them, she wasn't sure what outcome she would prefer.

With Kral close behind, she went to the door of Lupinius's room. He had not been sleeping well, so she was afraid he would be awake inside, or at least sleeping only lightly. But there was nothing for it. She had to go in.

She opened his door as quietly as she could and stepped inside. The room was dark, but she knew immediately that it was empty. There was no sound of steady breathing, none of her uncle's masculine scent.

To make sure, she went to his bed. Nothing.

She turned back to Kral. "He is not here."

"Have you a lantern?" Kral asked. "If he is away, we can search his room better with some light."

She told him to wait there and hurried to her own room to fetch hers. She kept it on a bureau in her room, along with a few prized possessions she had brought in from her father's house: a silver comb, her mother's bejeweled mirror, the copper armband that Kral had given her.

But when she turned up the flame slightly, she realized that the mirror was gone.

She gasped audibly, almost dropping the lantern.

Where could it have gone, she wondered? The only time she had taken it anywhere was the one time she had shown it to Kral. She was already staying in this house by then, because her father was away on his mission. She had brought it back here and never taken it away since. And she remembered having glanced at it before going to bed.

Had Kral come into her room while she slept?

She turned, and he was already in her doorway. "I heard a noise," he said. "Is everything all right?"

She fixed him with a steady, stern gaze. "Did you come in here, before I woke up?" she asked.

"No. The room you found me in was the first one I searched. I entered through a window there."

"My mirror is missing," she revealed. "The one I showed you, remember?"

"Yes," Kral said immediately. "And you did not put it somewhere else?"

"I left it next to the lantern, before bed."

He looked on the bureau, then squatted and looked behind it, between the massive chest and the wall. Seeing nothing, he turned and checked under and around the bed.

"It's just gone," she said.

Kral shrugged. "Bring the lantern," he suggested. "We can search your uncle's room."

Alanya felt unsettled by the discovery—by everything that had happened in the last several minutes, she realized. Finding him in her house, alive and unharmed, learning that he was the Ghost of the Wall, the killer so many feared. Then finding her uncle missing from his bed and her mirror from its place in her room.

She didn't put a lot of stock in portents, but something was very wrong.

She handed Kral the lantern and followed him back to

Lupinius's room. He held it high when they arrived there, and scanned the whole room quickly.

It only took Alanya a moment to realize that things had changed, though.

"He is gone," she announced.

"Gone? What do you mean?"

She pointed out things usually in place that were now missing. "He always keeps his sword and his boots by his bed at night," she said.

"Perhaps he is out at the wall."

"He could be," she agreed. "But then, why would the trunk on which they rest be gone as well?"

"He took a trunk?" Kral asked.

She quickly looked around the room for other signs. Some of his clothing was gone from his wardrobe, and though he usually kept an assortment of weapons close at hand, none were visible.

"He's gone," she stated flatly. "Not gone from the house—gone. From Koronaka."

"He cannot be," Kral argued.

"He is. He packed up his most important things in his trunk, and took them."

"And the Teeth?"

"Your crown?" Alanya asked. "I don't see it."

"Could he have taken your mirror?" Kral asked.

The thought had not occurred to her, but now she realized that he was right. Lupinius was well aware of the mirror, having admired it—and commented on the probable value of its gemstones—several times since she had brought it into his house. "He might have."

She was about to say more when a movement from outside the room captured her attention. Kral's hand dropped to his waist and came up with a knife in it, but Alanya stayed his arm.

"What's going on?" Donial asked. He wore a light gray nightshirt, and his dark hair stuck up at every angle. His eyes were puffy with sleep. "Why are you in here—and you," he said to the Pict. At the sight of Kral his eyes widened, alertness flooding into him. His body coiled, ready to run or strike. "What are *you* doing here? I'll call the Rangers."

"No!" Alanya said firmly. "This is Kral, my friend. And look—Uncle Lupinius is gone! He has slipped away, like a thief. More than like one—he stole the mirror that belonged to our mother."

"I do not believe it," Donial said. "Let me wake Calvert. He'll know."

"It is true, Donial," Alanya insisted. "Look for yourself. His trunk is gone, his favorite clothing, his gear."

"How do you know your 'friend' did not murder him?" Donial challenged. "That looks like blood on him."

"I would have, but I never had the chance," Kral countered. "He was gone when I arrived."

"Why would he . . . why would he leave us?" Donial asked. Alanya felt sorry for her brother, as the weight of her revelation began to impact him. "Does he not—?"

"What?" Alanya asked. "Does he not love us? He never did. Does he trust us? Not a bit. He got our father killed, remember, with his foolish expedition. He took us in reluctantly. I don't believe he would hesitate for a moment to leave us far behind."

"But he . . . he is our father's brother," Donial said. *He can't bring himself to admit the truth,* Alanya thought. She and her brother were nothing but burdens to Lupinius. Burdens he had never asked for and didn't want.

"Donial," Alanya said seriously, "you must trust me. Lupinius is gone. Kral did nothing to him. But we are alone now, and Lupinius has stolen from us—"

"And from me," Kral interjected. "From my people."

"So we are on our own, brother. Like it or not, we are alone now."

18

THE THREE OF them had moved into Lupinius's office, so Kral could close the window by which he had entered. He had spotted guards outside, but had easily eluded them. He'd been doing that most of the night, since leaving the barracks in which he had learned Lupinius's name. He had chosen a couple of other victims, closer to the town, and from one had learned—after some less-than-gentle persuasion—where the man named Lupinius was and that he had been both a prime instigator as well as the military commander of the invasion of the Bear Clan village.

Which only made sense. As the commander, he would have been in a position to claim the Teeth if he wanted.

So Kral had made his way to Lupinius's house, then inside. He'd been startled to find Alanya there. Surely she had mentioned her uncle, but if she'd ever said his name, he didn't remember it. So many of those Aquilonian names sounded similar, to him, so when she spoke the names of people in the fort, he had paid scant attention.

At first, his reflex had been to kill her as soon as he saw

her. But he could not bring himself to do that. He knew, in his heart, that she had not betrayed him.

Now they sat in Lupinius's chairs; he, Alanya, and her little brother Donial—who, by his manner, Kral suspected might have been the one who *had* betrayed him. He knew the night was wasting away, and with morning's light, escape would be much harder. But he hadn't been able to force himself to leave yet.

"What will you do now?" Alanya asked him.

He didn't even have to think about it. "Go after him."

"After Uncle Lupinius?" Donial asked, surprised.

"Of course," Kral said. "He has taken the crown. I must return it to its rightful place. I have no choice."

"How will you find him?" Alanya wondered.

"He's traveling through the forest. He will leave tracks."

"And if he's taken the road, instead?"

"There will still be tracks," Kral said. He knew following Lupinius's trail was the least of his worries. Anyone who would take a trunk with him when fleeing would not be hard to find.

But Alanya surprised him with her next announcement. "Then you will not go alone, Kral."

"What do you mean?"

"I mean, Donial and I will accompany you."

"You cannot," Kral responded.

"Why?"

The reasons were legion, he knew. They would slow him down. They would not be as stealthy in the forests as a Pict and would expose him to danger. If he had to worry about where they were, he might be less careful himself.

"I travel alone," he said, as if that explained it all.

"You used to," Alanya said.

"Why do you want to come?"

Donial sat watching the whole exchange with a confused expression on his face. He would go wherever his sister said, Kral supposed. "Lupinius stole from us as well as from you," Alanya reminded him. "That mirror is my only memento of my mother, and now my father as well. And if Father had anything else of worth that he meant for us to have, Lupinius has no doubt taken that, too. If he could fit Father's estate into his trunk, he would doubtless do so. Anyway, he wouldn't have run like a frightened rat if he was not guilty of something, would he? I suspect he had a hand in our father's death. Perhaps more than a hand."

"And you, Donial?" Kral asked. The young man still eyed him with suspicion, as if Kral might decide at any moment to plunge that knife into his heart. "How do you feel about it?"

Donial looked uncertain, his gaze flitting back and forth between Kral and his sister. "I . . ." he began. Then he closed his mouth again and gave a small shrug. Kral thought the boy wanted to cry, but he fought back his tears.

"Donial stays with me," Alanya announced firmly.

Kral didn't usually like to think for too long on any given topic. He knew that if he declined to take them along, they could make all sorts of trouble for him. They could alert the soldiers to his presence now, before he even left the town. And if he did get away, they could set troops on his trail.

He could kill them.

Or he could take them along.

One thing was certain. Lupinius would not have gone west, deeper into Pictish territory, or north, into Cimmeria. No, he would be traveling back into Aquilonia.

Having Aquilonian allies, who knew the language well and understood the customs, might come in handy.

Anyway, if he hadn't been able to kill Alanya at that first moment, when the bloodlust had been hot within him and the fear of discovery strong, he wouldn't be able to do it now.

"Very well," he said. "But we leave now. With every hour that passes, he gets farther ahead of us."

"Now?" Donial repeated.

"Now."

"We'll dress quickly," Alanya countered. "And then we'll go. Kral, see if you can find some provisions in the pantry for our journey. And mind you do not wake the staff."

Kral cocked his head and looked at her. His Aquilonian was still rudimentary, and he wasn't sure he understood her tone of voice.

But it sounded as if she was giving him orders. He had only just decided not to kill her, and here she was telling him what to do.

Still, what she said made perfect sense. And it was her house, or her uncle's.

He decided he might as well go along with her, at least for the moment. Where was the harm in that?

WITH EVERY MILE he put behind him, Lupinius felt better and better. He was under Aquilonian skies again. Koronaka was still more fresh than a nightmare, but getting farther away all the time. The day had dawned bright and warm, like the new life he headed toward. Compared to Koronaka, Tarantia seemed like a distant paradise. He would be safe from Sharzen's wrath there, if the fool dared to express it. Sharzen would be terrified to show himself in the king's capital city. But Conan, even if he was angry at Sharzen, would have no way of knowing Lupinius's role in the raid on the Bear Clan. He would be the sorrowful brother, still mourning the loss of Conan's ambassador. Perhaps King Conan would even reward him for his loss.

With his horse moving steadily beneath him, Lupinius glanced over at Calvert, riding alongside his wagon. When he had learned that the Ghost of the Wall was hunting for him—on top of everything else that had gone wrong—he had summoned Calvert and told him to choose a dozen of his bravest, most loyal Rangers. He packed his trunk, and while some of Calvert's Rangers distracted the guards sent over by Sharzen, the rest loaded the wagon. With most of the city's soldiers assigned to the western walls, it was a simple matter to set out for the east.

They traveled all of that first night, and as morning grew brighter, they were still on the march, trying to put as much distance between themselves and Koronaka as possible. None of the Rangers had any loyalty to Governor Sharzen, except to the extent that they were loyal to Aquilonia's king and his appointed subjects. But Lupinius paid them, and like most warriors, their allegiance went first to the man who filled their hands with gold.

Calvert, muscular and handsome, tossed Lupinius an easy grin. "A new day dawns, eh?" he said.

"That's right," Lupinius agreed. "Brighter than the last."

"I just hope the wall holds behind us," Calvert said, with a chuckle. "Long enough for us to reach civilization, at any rate."

"It will hold for a while," Lupinius speculated. "But if Sharzen keeps putting all his resources into it while the rest of the settlements do nothing, it may ultimately make Koronaka weaker, not stronger. Were I a Pict war chief, that is where I would attack."

"I'm glad you are not," Calvert announced. "Rather would I ride in your company into Tarantia than into that forsaken wilderness again."

Lupinius nodded. "Especially since we ride toward my brother's estate there—or should I say, my estate, by right of blood?"

"From the way you describe it, Lupinius, I suspect we will find comfort there."

Lupinius didn't much care for the way Calvert spoke to him—almost as an equal rather than as an employee. That was new. Until last night, Calvert had always shown him the appropriate respect. Something had changed. Lupinius supposed it was that Calvert understood they were becoming outlaws, after a fashion, or at least behaving like them. Sneaking away from the town in the dead of night, carrying what booty they could, and leaving the rest of the Rangers, as well as the household staff and his brother's useless spawn, to fend for themselves. They had become conspirators together, accomplices in something that felt like a crime, although in fact it was not. Lupinius wasn't sure he liked this new order, but there was little he could do about it without risking Calvert's wrath. And he didn't want to make this journey without the Rangers—the bandit Khatak was on the loose, according to reports, as were other brigands.

He was safer than in Koronaka, but until he was inside the walls of his new home in Tarantia, he would not rest easy.

What he hadn't told Calvert, or anyone else, was that he still had the foul souvenir he'd taken from the Pict village, the crown of bones and teeth. He still had to believe, based on the way it was protected, that it had mystical significance. Back in Tarantia, he knew of a mage who could help him determine its true value, if any. Perhaps the mage would even buy it himself, if it was important enough.

Even if that failed to produce any notable income, he had also taken his niece's mirror, the gems of which would bring a pretty penny. And, of course, his brother's estate had lands and possessions. If only he had thought of this earlier, he could have spared himself time and trouble, sitting in Koronaka waiting for King Conan to make the intelligent decision on funding the wall.

MUCH TO KRAL'S chagrin, they were unavoidably delayed in setting off after Lupinius. Donial found it amusing—the Pict had been so anxious to get on the road, then he was the one who stalled them. He actually had

Donial and Alanya spend the rest of the night in a clearing
in the woods, less than three miles from Koronaka's eastern
gate, while he went dashing back across the Black to tell his
fellow savages that he was leaving. They took advantage of
the time to sleep for a while. By the time Kral reached them
again, it was morning.

Still, the way he had taken them out of Uncle Lupinius's
place and past the guards had been impressive. He may
have been a savage, but he was as quick and agile as a cat,
and he seemed to have a knack for finding the shadowed
places where one could hide.

When he rejoined them, shortly after first light, Kral
had a smile on his face. He walked with the springy step of
one who hadn't been awake and running around all night
long. With him he brought three horses, a chestnut and a
dun mare, and a red roan stallion with a white blaze on his
muzzle. All three were saddled and bridled, ready to ride.

"Where did you get those?" Alanya asked with a laugh.
Her long hair was loose, and she wore a simple brown tunic, riding breeches, and buckskin boots. Donial's outfit
was similar, but his tunic was green, and he had a sword
hanging from his belt. He wasn't about to leave their defense entirely up to the savage.

"From some soldiers who didn't need them as much as
we do," Kral said. The blood, and much of the blue paint,
had been washed off by his trips across the river. His hair
and the skin he wore as a loincloth had dried, and he
looked almost clean, for a Pict.

"Do they know that?"

"They will," Kral said. "But by the time they count, we
will be long gone."

Alanya looked at him admiringly. "What else have you
been doing?" she asked him. For his part, Donial still had a
hard time coming up with a civil sentence for the Pict, or
imagining why he should. But Alanya clearly liked him
and trusted him.

"Arranging for Klea to keep up my efforts," Kral replied.

"What efforts?" Alanya asked.

"Harassing the settlers. Slowing progress on the wall. Trying to find the Teeth."

"I thought Lupinius had the crown," Alanya said, confused.

"We think he does," Kral answered. "We don't know that for certain. Until we do, I do not want to let up on the fort."

"So even though we're taking you away, there will continue to be a Ghost of the Wall?"

"There will," Kral said, with a broad grin. He helped Alanya up into her saddle on the dun. The chestnut mare was to be for Donial, and Kral would ride the roan. "Those who slaughtered the Bear Clan, breaking the agreed truce, will continue to pay for their crimes."

"To be fair," Donial pointed out as he mounted the chestnut, "you Picts are the enemy."

"To be fair," Kral countered, "when two enemies are in a state of truce, they are not exactly enemies. Or at least, they are not supposed to be fighting."

"I suppose that's true," Donial said.

"It is," Alanya confirmed. "That's what Father always told us—that we were safe from Pict attacks because we had a truce with the Bear Clan."

"And then the Picts killed him," Donial observed.

"We know not who killed him," Alanya said. "We have only Uncle's version of that story, and I no longer trust him in the least."

"If a Pict did kill your father, it is because he was part of the attacking force," Kral suggested. "Of course they tried to defend their homes."

Donial, remembering the soldier who had claimed Father's wound was too large to have been made by a Pictish spear, had no argument for that. "I knew others who died, friends of mine," Donial said. "Do not expect me to forget that, Kral."

"Donial!" Alanya shouted, a horrified look on her face. Donial felt a moment's shame—if he had done something wrong, he didn't know what, but his sister was sure acting like he had.

"Worry not, Alanya," Kral said. "And Donial, I do not expect you to forget, any more than I expect to forget my family and friends who died in the attack. There are three left, of my whole village, Donial. Three. I will never forget that."

"Are you going to murder us in our sleep?" Donial asked.

"If I was going to do that, I would have done so last night," Kral pointed out. "It would have been far easier to get out of town safely without the two of you."

"He has a point," Alanya noted.

"No one says we have to like each other, Donial," Kral added. "But if we're to travel together, we must try to trust each other."

Trusting a savage, and one of the same clan that had killed his father, seemed like a tall order. But Donial understood the point that Kral was making. If they couldn't trust one another, this temporary partnership would never work at all.

He would try, then. He would keep an eye on Kral, but he would try to let the Pict prove himself as trustworthy.

And, he thought, as he prodded his mount into an easy trot, he would turn him in to Aquilonian authorities at the first possible opportunity.

19

THEY WERE ATTACKED on the second day.

Lupinius had no way of knowing if they were being pursued. But if the Ghost of the Wall had really chosen him as the object of his murderous wrath, he didn't want to take unnecessary chances. He allowed the horses and the small band of Rangers that accompanied him to take short rests from time to time, and a few hours of sleep on the second night, but they had been going for two nights and part of another day, and all were weary.

It was almost noon. The early-autumn sun was high and merciless. The riders had shed helmets and mail and rode in loose tunics, wetting cloths to wrap about their heads or necks from time to time to help stave off the heat. Months in the cooler climes of the Westermarck had lowered their tolerance for the heat of the inland valleys through which they rode.

Lupinius was nodding off, almost asleep at the wagon's reins, when three riders stepped their horses onto the narrow road. Sheer cliff walls rose up on one side of the roadway.

The other was clotted with low trees and scrub, thorny and dense. The trees had been tall enough to conceal the riders, though. The men were armored, with helmets that covered their faces. One of them held a crossbow, the others straight swords of medium length and breadth.

Calvert, who usually rode close to Lupinius, moved instead to the head of the column and hailed the riders.

"Move off the road," he commanded. "We would pass."

"In good time," the rider in the center answered. His voice was gruff, and the sword he held remained visibly displayed.

"What is the meaning of this?" Lupinius demanded. Around him, Rangers freed swords from scabbards. Trey, mounted just ahead of him, slipped his longbow off his back and plucked an arrow from a quiver. The mood of the day had gone from lazy and sleepy to bowstring taut in an instant. Even the birds overhead seemed to have quieted.

"No one needs be hurt," the apparent leader of the riders said. "We can see by your escort, sir, and your bearing, that you are a man of some distinction. All we want, then, are the contents of that wagon. The lot of you can keep your horses and ride on."

Calvert couldn't contain a sputter of laughter. "Three of you against ten Rangers?"

"Your count, not mine," the rider said. Uneasy, Lupinius tilted his head and looked up the cliff wall that flanked the road. Staggered among the boulders there were at least twenty men. Some had arrows drawn and pointed down, others had massive rocks in their hands that they could send crashing down at a moment's notice. The ambushers had picked their spot well. The road was too narrow here to allow for easy retreat, especially with the wagon. They could probably charge through the three men blocking the road, but who knew if there were more back in those trees and scrub? And they would certainly take heavy casualties from those stationed above.

By giving up the wagon, Lupinius could probably save his own skin—if these brigands were to be taken at their word. And in their defense, they could have simply attacked first, rather than making such a demand, if they intended to kill Lupinius and the Rangers anyway. Which made the calculation a little more difficult. If he had been sure they'd die anyway, he would have just insisted they fight their way out.

All this went through his mind in a matter of seconds. Calvert had partially turned on his mount to see what Lupinius's decision might be, but hadn't turned his back completely on the three riders. Finally, Lupinius decided that fighting was the best course. He gave Calvert a discreet nod.

The Ranger exploded into action. He wheeled and struck out with his sword at the leader of the three riders. Trey, the Bossonian, let an arrow fly, catching the second rider between helm and breastplate. The outlaw flew from his horse and landed hard in the dirt.

From above, shafts rained down toward the Rangers. Three stuck into the wagon, not far from where Lupinius sat. But he whipped the drawing horses into a frenzy and egged them lurching onward.

The third rider loosed a crossbow bolt that slammed into a Ranger's breast, knocking him from his mount with a spray of crimson gore. Another Ranger fell under a boulder hurled from the cliff's face. A third went down with two arrows jutting from his back like quills.

Lupinius kept the horses pulling the wagon on the road and moving forward. Ahead, Calvert and the leader of the brigands were trading sword blows. Sparks flew when their blades clashed, and the clang of steel against steel echoed off the cliff wall. Lupinius didn't want to run over his own man, but the arrows from above were coming dangerously close, so he bore down anyway.

Before he reached the battling horsemen, however, a jolt to his wagon caused him to spin in his seat. One of the brigands had jumped from the wall and advanced unsteadily on him. The man was helmeted, like the rest, but his mail shirt was worn and ragged, and his blade nicked from dozens of battles.

Lupinius released the reins and hastily drew his own sword from its place in the wagon's boot. He brought it up just in time to block the brigand's downward swing. The motion of the wagon's bed made it hard for him to stand, reducing the amount of force he could get behind his swing. Lupinius, parrying from a seated position, put more power into his. The other man staggered backward. Lupinius didn't dare pursue him into the wagon's bed, but pawed for the reins while keeping his attention riveted on his assailant.

When the man composed himself enough to make a second try, Lupinius jerked the reins, bringing the horses suddenly short. The brigand's legs went out from under him again, this time tossing him forward. Lupinius slashed upward at the same moment, and his sword bit cleanly through the brigand's sternum, splashing Lupinius with hot blood.

The man's corpse fell toward Lupinius, who shoved it off the wagon. He tried to bring the horses under control at the same time. He was almost on top of Calvert, who still matched the robbers' leader blow for blow. At the last moment, he was able to nudge the horses away from Calvert and his opponent, racing past the battling men. The brigand's steed reared back as the wagon rumbled past it. Calvert wheeled his horse into the other while it was off-balance. The outlaw's horse fell over on its side, sending the outlaw leader flying.

Calvert leapt down from his own mount and ran to where the brigand was trying to recover from the spill. Showing no quarter, Calvert cleaved him from shoulder blade to stomach before the man could regain his footing.

Lupinius kept the wagon charging forward at full speed, beyond the last of the outlaws. He glanced back when he felt he could afford to take his gaze away from the road ahead. A severely depleted Ranger force rode toward him, away from the ambush. Calvert yet lived, as did Trey, Constantus, Rufio, Ondene, and Kelvan. Four had fallen to the brigands' attack.

Lupinius's heart pounded in his chest as he drove the horses on. Calvert and the other Rangers spurred their mounts onward, catching up shortly. Calvert rode alongside, his face still flushed with the effort of battle and the thrill of victory. "Who were they?" Lupinius asked him.

"I don't know," Calvert admitted breathlessly. "At first . . . at first I thought it was Khatak and his rogues, as they haunt this region. But if it had been Khatak, I doubt we'd be speaking now, unless it was at the gates of hell."

"If not him, then some other like him," Lupinius said, beginning to calm a little at last. "That was good work, back there."

"Aye," Calvert agreed. "Not good enough, though. We lost four good men, and brave Rangers all. I would go back for their bodies if we dared."

"Too many of the scoundrels," Lupinius declared. "They would finish us if we went back for more."

"Likely," Calvert said. "We keep riding."

ALANYA WAS AFRAID that she was slowing Kral down, but he kept reassuring her. "We need not catch your uncle today or tomorrow," he insisted. "Sooner or later, he will come to rest. Good enough we catch him then."

After that first day's ride, she had wanted some time out of the saddle. Her bottom wasn't used to riding all day long. They had stopped in a pleasant river valley, Kral insisting they make their camp well away from the road, and they had spent the night underneath the stars.

Early in the morning, Kral had roused them. Alanya woke quickly, Donial with more resistance. But Kral had

already been up long enough to catch a large bird of some
kind and roast it on a spit over a campfire. They had eaten
only some bread and dried meat brought from Lupinius's
kitchen the day before, so the aroma of the bird set her
stomach roaring.

They were back on the road shortly. Alanya ached even
more today than the day before, she thought, but had no
choice other than to keep riding. She swore that once this
journey was over she would never again spend an entire
day on horseback.

The landscape they covered changed regularly throughout the day. They crossed low mountain ranges separated
by wide valleys. The trees went from being predominantly
pines and spreading oaks to a wider variety, including
spruce, ash, maple, and other types that she didn't know
the names of. Their leaves were a riot of colors, reds and
golds and browns, like swatches of bright fabric strewn
over the landscape. In the valleys, grasslands predomi-
nated, and the farther east they got the more likely they
were to see herds of animals browsing there—wild ones,
such as elk or deer, as well as domestic sheep and cattle.
They began to see occasional farmhouses as well.

Overhead, the sky was blue and nearly cloudless, and
the sun bore down on them with a ferocity she had almost
forgotten. Alanya was a creature of the city, where she
could always go inside under a roof to escape the sun, or
take a cooling dip at the nearest public baths. Even in Koronaka she had spent most of her time inside, and the air
had been cooler there.

As the day wore on, the sun and the scenery and the
steady, repetitive motion of the horse lulled her into a kind
of drowsy comfort. She talked now and again to Kral,
telling him of life in Aquilonia and what he might expect if
the chase took them as far as Tarantia. Donial was quiet.
She couldn't tell if he was being a sullen adolescent or just
exhausted from the journey. She didn't think he had slept

much the night before, but had stayed awake, starting at
every night noise.

She didn't really recognize the country they traversed
because she had only made the trip once before, while heading in the other direction. She knew they were on the same
road, the main thoroughfare from Tarantia to the Westermarck. Soon enough they would be nearing real civilization
again. One more mountain range to cross. Or maybe two.

They were riding away from the huge, flaming ball of
the setting sun when they came across the bodies.

Kral rode in the lead, and he reined up when he spotted
them. He glanced back at Alanya, his face clouded with
concern, as if he didn't want her to see them. But she was
too close behind and had noticed what he was looking at
almost as soon as he saw them.

"Those are—" she began.

"Corpses," Kral confirmed. They had been stripped bare
and tossed by the side of the road like abandoned chunks
of raw meat. Vultures had already been digging at them.
Alanya's stomach turned at the sight. Trying to imagine the
violence that had occurred here left her feeling dizzy and
sick.

"Who would have done this?" she asked.

Kral took a moment to answer, probably trying to remember the words. "Highwaymen, bandits," he said.

Donial caught up then, and Alanya tried to put her horse
between him and the bodies. "Don't look, Donial," she
urged him. "It's awful."

But his youthful curiosity got the better of him, and he
craned to peer past her. His face blanched. "I know them!"
he cried.

"No," Alanya said reflexively. "You can't."

"That's Pollonius," Donial insisted. "And Trellin. And
those others are familiar, too. They're all Rangers!"

Alanya forced herself to look again, to see beyond the
blood and the wounds, and she realized that he was right. She

had seen those faces before, in Koronaka, and in her uncle's employ. "We have to see if there are more!" she shouted.

Kral glared at her. "Quiet!" he snapped. "We have to get out of here. If the ones who did this are still around . . ."

"But what if Uncle Lupinius is nearby, maybe injured?" she asked. Knowing that wouldn't necessarily have much impact on Kral, she added, "What if he was robbed, and the thieves took the crown you're looking for?"

She could tell when the idea struck home. Kral's anxious stare suddenly changed, his forehead wrinkling, his eyes narrowing. "Quickly," he said. "We can look around, but quickly. If they come back, we're dead."

20

THE SUN WOULD set before too long, and Kral didn't want to be anywhere near the cliffs when it did. He could envision the whole scene in his head. Men hidden up among the rocks above, waiting for the Rangers to come along. They probably blocked off the road ahead, pinning the Rangers down between cliffs and trees, then opened fire from above. Others probably streamed out of the brush, and before the Rangers knew it they were overwhelmed, dragged from their horses, heads split open, throats cut.

At least, that was the way he would have done it.

Searching the immediate area, they found no more bodies, so Kral assumed that these were the only victims. Their bodies had been dragged to a central point, stripped and looted, then tossed off to the side for the jackals and carrion birds. The bandits had probably carried off their own dead, leaving only their victims to mark the spot and terrorize future travelers.

Kral glanced at the position of the sun again, just starting to sink over the distant mountain range. If terror had been the bandits' goal, it was working. Dying in battle didn't especially scare him. It was the noblest way a Pict could fall, and would guarantee him safe passage to the Mountains of the Dead. But he didn't want to see Alanya captured or killed. And he didn't want to die before he was able to restore the Teeth to its proper place in the Ice Bear's cave.

Finally, he summoned Alanya and Donial together. "Your uncle is not here," Kral said. "There are only those four bodies. That means the rest escaped. If Lupinius had fallen, he would be here with them."

"Unless they took him captive."

"I doubt that bandits like these take prisoners," Kral replied. Looking at Alanya, he didn't add the observation that they didn't take male captives, but might change their minds for a young, golden-haired beauty.

There was always a chance that Lupinius had ransomed his life with the Teeth, and whatever other treasure he had looted before leaving Koronaka. Kral hoped that wasn't the case. He couldn't follow both the bandits and Lupinius. If he made the wrong choice, the Teeth might be lost forever.

He decided to stay on Lupinius's trail. It was by far the safer bet. Once he had caught up with the man, if it turned out he had made the wrong choice, he could leave Alanya and Donial in the arms of civilization, where they belonged, and come back here after the thieves.

He swung himself up into his saddle. He knew Alanya was hurting from the days of riding, and he was more than a little sore himself. Traveling on horseback was not common for Picts, and he knew he'd need to build up some calluses before he was truly comfortable in the saddle. "We need to go," he declared.

"But . . ."

"He is not here, Alanya."

She looked crestfallen. Had she secretly hoped that they would find her uncle's body there? It would save her the discomfort of confronting him personally, Kral supposed. And it would make the rest of the trip easier.

But it wasn't to be. Resigned, she climbed back up on her mount, and Donial did the same. Kral didn't want to have to force them to ride through the dark of night, but he wanted some distance from this pile of rocks before he dared try to sleep.

MANG WALKED ALL that day and the next one, finally clambering up the steep, rocky slopes of a nearby mountain that the Picts called Talking Hill. There were many sacred spots in the Pict pantheon. As a people, they were close to the earth and took spiritual solace in her many moods. On Talking Hill, there was a spot where the Pictish ancestors, it was said, answered questions of the holy ones, the shamans. Mang was no shaman. But he had questions and didn't know how else to get them answered, without confiding to some other clan's shaman that crucial knowledge had been lost.

He knew about the sacred spot, though not where it was. Every Bear Clan Pict did, since it figured in many of their songs and stories. It was on the side of the mountain that faced the setting sun, halfway up, inside a circle of standing gray stones, in the shade of a tall, twisted tree. He began to wonder if he would ever find it, on the side of such a great hill as this. But presently his path intersected a series of stone steps, twined with native grasses and covered in lichens and soil so that they might have been carved from the face of the mountain itself. Mang started up them. They were smooth, worn down by the feet of hundreds of generations of Pictish shamans.

Finally, the steps led toward the twisted tree, standing by itself on a bluff. Once he had reached the correct level it was an easy matter to find the circle of stones. They were jet-black and polished to a glassy sheen, half the height of a man, and must have taken the work of many strong warriors to position in this way.

Unless it was the work of the gods.

Along the way, he found himself worrying about Klea from time to time. She had agreed to carry on Kral's efforts, hampering the construction of the wall at every turn. The first night after Kral had left on his quest, she had gone to the wall to do that. Just before first light she had returned, energized and enthusiastic. She had been able to upend a new section that had been started but had not yet set, and she had fired three flaming arrows over the wall. When she had returned to find Mang sitting up waiting for her, she had broken into raucous laughter, describing the antics of the settlers trying to find her in the woods. Her blue paint was smeared from rivers and woods, but her spirits were high.

Mang had left then, confident that she would be able to keep herself safe and make life hard on their enemies at the same time. Besides, he had important things to do, too. He carried a bow and a knife, dressed in a loincloth with a fur wrap across his chest and shoulders, and wore hide sandals on his feet. His long, graying hair was tied back with a leather thong.

Now, outside the circle of strange stones, he put his weapons down on the ground, shook off the wrap, tugged away the loincloth and sandals. One entered the circle naked as the gods made you, or not at all.

Once inside, however, he wasn't sure what to do. He was no holy man. He sat on the earth, as bare of leaves, weeds, and grass as if someone had raked it clean, and rested his hands on his knees. After about twenty minutes had passed with nothing at all happening, he decided to speak out loud.

"I need to know about the Teeth of the Ice Bear," he said. "What happens if it is away from the cave and in the world of man? What happens if the crown of Teeth is lost?"

He sat for so long that he began to despair of ever get-
ting the answers he sought. As the eldest survivor of the
Bear Clan, looking after the Teeth was his responsibility.
He had to find out somehow what it was all about.

Mang wasn't sure when the landscape around him
started to change. It was subtle at first, barely noticeable. A
difference in the quality of the light. A thinning of the at-
mosphere, maybe. The green of tree leaves became richer,
a shade darker. The dirt on which he sat grew darker brown,
more saturated. Even the sunlight felt a little warmer on his
naked flesh.

But then, at almost the same moment that Mang noticed
things were changing around him, the change grew more
dramatic. Instead of getting warmer, the temperature
dropped dramatically as an icy wind blew up, seemingly
confined within the circle of standing stones. Outside the
circle, everything blurred into liquid masses of color with
no definable shape, while inside, Mang could see every
pebble, every speck of dirt, with absolute crystal clarity.
His chest tightened with fear, his hands clenching, nails
digging into his skin.

And then even that changed, and Mang no longer sat on
the mountainside. He didn't seem to be anywhere in particular, to have any physical form at all. He was all senses—
skin tingling with some invisible power, nose filled with
out-of-place smells of pine sap and mint and the rich,
earthy stink of a bush hog, ears rattled by winds and a
high-pitched humming, tongue tasting the fresh bite of an
apple, of all things.

And his eyes . . . his eyes were full of images that
couldn't be real, that he couldn't truly be seeing. With what
little self-awareness he could muster in that moment of
dizzying strangeness, he wondered if he had gone mad. He
saw—or believed he saw—the Ice Bear itself, massive and
monstrous, its slavering jaw open, revealing huge, razor-
like teeth. The thing walked with its head swaying before

it, enormous shoulders moving under a coat of frosted white fur as thick and deep as the trees coating the side of a mountain. Icicles the size of inverted trees dangled from its thick coat. Its gigantic feet smashed forests flat with every stride. Its bulk was vast enough to block out the sun for miles. Around it swirled killing winds: winds that iced over the rivers, froze and destroyed the fields and the forests, and left hapless humans dead in their wake.

Mang watched the Ice Bear devastate villages. He could feel the mournful wailing of those left behind, the terror of those who witnessed its implacable approach with nowhere to run or hide.

And then, as he watched, a Pict who seemed somehow taller and stronger than the rest approached the gigantic creature. This Pict stood straight and tall, and Mang had a sense that incredible power emanated from him. As it approached, the Ice Bear seemed to shudder with surprise at this tiny being who didn't run from it.

Instead, the Pict spoke words Mang couldn't hear, and waved sticks that he couldn't quite make out but must have been magic items of great import. The Ice Bear's huge maw snapped closed, and its eyes grew wide with fear. It tried to turn and run, but the man—no bigger than a flea, in comparison with a regular bear—held his ground and continued to work his magic.

And the impossible happened. Under the brave Pict's spell, the Ice Bear slumped helplessly to the ground, filling in most of a wide valley with his bulk. The bear's eyes closed, its head turned, its tongue lolled out of its open mouth.

Incredibly, the Pict threw down his magic sticks, stepped inside that mouth, and began to wrench the teeth loose with his hands. As he pried each one loose he threw it outside the mouth. When he was done, he climbed back out and picked them up. Only as soon as the teeth had hit the ground, they had shrunk. From this vantage point, Mang could barely see them, could only tell that the man had a handful of them.

Time started to move at a faster pace then. The body of the Ice Bear stayed where it was. Somehow, Mang knew that it was not dead, but only slumbering, as deeply asleep as if mesmerized. Dirt blew up against the body and covered it, then trees grew on the dirt, and grass, and people came and built huts and villages there, and Mang knew that the Ice Bear had become another range of hills on which Picts could live.

He saw the Pict again, working the teeth he had yanked and some bones into the crown he knew as the Teeth of the Ice Bear. When it was finished, the Pict put it on his own head. He walked into a cave, and Mang understood that this was the first Guardian, taking the Teeth into the cave where it would be safe. At the same time, though he could not have said how, Mang knew that removing the Teeth from the cave—and the care of a Guardian—would be disastrous. The Ice Bear would wake, would roam the world once again. His sheer size, combined with the frost and the rimy winds that accompanied him, would spread new havoc upon the earth.

With this realization, Mang felt his stomach lurch as if he were falling back to the ground from some impossible height. He was back in the circle of standing black stones, back where he had been before everything had changed. The sun was warm on his skin, but lower in the sky. He couldn't tell for sure how much time had passed, but a couple of hours, at least.

He waited in the circle a few more minutes, to see if anything else would happen. When it didn't, he rose and left it, donning his clothing again and picking up his weapons.

He knew enough now, he was convinced.

Enough to know that if the Teeth wasn't restored to the Ice Bear's cave, disaster would ensue.

He didn't want that responsibility on his head. And he definitely did not want to live through the second coming of the Ice Bear.

He started down the hill again, anxious to tell Klea what he had learned.

21

KRAL COULD HARDLY believe his eyes.

Alanya had spent the last several days, as they traveled, telling him stories of Tarantia. Donial, too; as they neared the city of his birth, he became more vocal, more enthusiastic about their return. He seemed to forget his grudge against Kral long enough to share that enthusiasm.

But the stories only spun webs of words, forming pictures in his mind that did not come near the reality that his astonished eyes beheld when Tarantia finally came into view.

Even before the city was in sight, there were miles of cultivated farmland, then small towns—"small" according to Alanya and Donial, but still larger than any Kral had ever imagined. Buildings of stone and timber, windows of glass, roofs of thatch. They continued on their way, with some of the people they passed staring at him, a Pict in the company of two Aquilonians, as if he were some kind of captive animal on display.

And then they topped a low rise, on the other side of

which Tarantia lay in a broad valley, gleaming like the most precious jewel in all creation. Its walls were as tall as the hill on which the Bear Clan's village had stood, the hill that they had thought so high that it could never be overrun. And even taller than the walls, shining towers caught the setting sun, spires sparkled as if ablaze.

The architecture was phenomenal enough, but perhaps more staggering was the sheer amount and variety of humanity Kral observed passing through the city's gates. He, Alanya, and Donial joined a veritable river of people—a double river, in fact, for just as many issued forth from the gates as headed into them. There were dark-skinned Kushites, and dusky Stygians, blond Brythunians and Gundermen, ruddy-faced, red-haired Vanirmen. And, of course, Aquilonians by the hundreds, wearing more different types of clothing than Kral had ever thought possible. Bright reds and yellows and blues. Soft purple robes, pantaloons of silk as white as snow, jerkins of tanned leather dyed colors never seen on a beast of field or forest.

Kral saw an old man in bright blue furs, and a young woman in a clingy yellow gauze that barely concealed her lush figure, walking side by side. He saw a merchant leading a team of mules who drew a wagon laden with fruits the likes of which Kral had never known could be harvested or even grown. He saw a trio of women playing musical instruments as they walked, which Alanya identified as a flute and a lyre and a small, dainty brass horn.

The procession of humanity in both directions raised a cloud of dust. Even though the roadway was paved, there were more people than the paving stones could accommodate, and many had to walk on the dirt at the sides of the road. Kral didn't mind, though he inhaled dust, because it was just another part of the spectacle.

"You never told me—" he began.

"I did," Alanya interrupted, laughing. "We did. You should see your face!"

"It's so much," Kral said. "There are more people on this bit of road than I've seen in my whole life."

"Because you spent all your time in that forsaken wilderness instead of getting out to see the world," Donial opined. Kral whirled to see if the youngster was mocking him, but Donial had a smile on his face. He looked like he was just in high spirits and not intentionally making fun. In good spirits himself, Kral decided to let it go.

Talking and laughing, they came nearer and nearer to the gates of the city. Kral's neck began to ache from craning his head to look at the heights of the walls and the towers beyond. At the gates, armed guards studied them, and Kral's hand dropped unconsciously to the knife at his hip. But he had donned clothing loaned him by Donial, and the guards made no move to stop or challenge them. And Alanya and Donial seemed to accept their perusal without comment. Kral followed suit.

Then they were inside the walls, and his amazement just grew more pronounced. Buildings were jammed together with a kind of manic energy. Lanes between them were narrow and packed with people, drayage carts, animals, and more. Merchants seemed to sell everything under the sun, and then some. It was growing dark, but lamps burning oil cast illumination onto the streets. Passersby jostled Kral when he slowed in the road, slack-jawed at the bustle and noise. "Is everyone in the world within these city walls?" he asked quietly.

"Not everyone," Alanya answered. "But the best people are."

"Some of the best," Kral countered. "Your uncle is here, too, we think." His trail had led them here, at any rate— up to the point that they lost it, on the road into Tarantia, where the sheer volume of traffic erased any track instantly.

"The best, and some of the worst," Alanya agreed.

"I never dreamed it was like this," Kral said. "How will

we ever find him, in all this? How does one even find his own home?"

"You get used to it," Donial replied. "You learn the streets in your neighborhood, and some of the bigger ones throughout the city. Some you never learn the names of, others you never see."

"And some you hope to avoid," Alanya added. "Especially at night."

"Why?" Kral wondered. "Is that where the beasts hunt?"

"The only beasts in Tarantia are work animals," Donial said. "Alanya refers to beasts of the human kind: robbers, murderers, scoundrels of every type."

"There are districts where they gamble and drink and carouse," Alanya explained. "Or so I've been told. I have never actually seen those parts of the city for myself."

"I have," Donial admitted. "On certain occasions when my friends and I went to explore that which we were warned against."

Alanya's face crimsoned, and Kral burst into laughter. "Donial!" she said.

"Easy, Alanya," Kral said. "Boys will find trouble wherever they live."

Alanya's laughter joined his, and she shook her head. "So will girls," she said after a moment. "I am just pleased that he never saw my friends and me there when he was doing his exploring."

Eventually, it occurred to Kral that Alanya and Donial really did know their way around, and were leading him in a particular direction. "Where are we going?" he asked.

"Home," Alanya answered.

"Home?" He thought of their home as being in Koronaka, even though they had lived here. He knew they had no living relatives here anymore.

"Our father has a house here," Donial said, his voice

catching at the mention of his late parent. "Since he's . . . since he's gone, it's ours now."

"In my village, if the owners of a hut were killed or gone for as long as you have been away from here, others would have moved in. There are always people marrying, after all, and needing new homes to live in."

"Look around you, Kral," Alanya said. "Does it look like there's a shortage of places for people to live? No, our father's house will be waiting for us. His household staff should be in it, keeping it for us against our return."

"Is it large enough for the three of us?" Kral asked.

"And thirty more," Alanya said. "Worry not, you'll share a bed with no one."

A bed. Kral had seen beds, since sneaking into Koronaka. But he had never slept in one, and wasn't sure he'd be able to. They seemed absurdly soft, not firm and unyielding like the ground he was used to.

Embarrassed, he glanced away from Alanya. If he were to share a bed with anyone, he knew, he would want it to be that golden-tressed lovely who he was so fortunate enough to ride beside.

But that was never going to happen. *It might have, once,* he thought. Before her people had attacked his clan, before her father had been killed, and his family and friends. The blood spilled that day was like a vast river between them, one that couldn't be bridged or swum. One could not reverse the course of a river; one could not turn back the tide of time, to make something not happen once it had.

So if he had to sleep in a bed, it would be alone.

Anyway, if no one was watching him, he could just as easily shove the bed aside and use the floor.

A short while later, in a quieter, less populous and boisterous section of the city, Alanya and Donial reined their horses up short. Kral glanced at them and saw that both their faces were clouded over, frown lines wrinkling their foreheads so identically that it was clear at that moment that they were brother and sister, despite the physical differences between them. He brought his own mount to a halt. "What is it?"

"Father's house," Alanya said. She nodded toward a structure on the other side of a wide square, and Kral looked to see what had bothered them both.

The house was larger than the one in which Lupinius had lived, back in Koronaka. White columns fronted it, and behind those, a wide gallery ran its length. Even before that, a fence, taller than the tallest man, encircled the entire building, so that Kral couldn't see much below the tops of the columns and gallery, could not see the doors at all. There were a few windows, curtained or shuttered against the night, and behind these, lights burned against the darkness.

"Huge," Kral noted.

"Not that," Alanya said. "Those guards."

Kral looked again. He had barely paid them any mind, so impressed was he with the size of the place. In front of the gate, illuminated by guttering torches, stood three guards wearing plate armor and black cloaks. Long swords dangled at their hips. Their faces were lean and fierce, with scars that told tales of battles fought and experience hard-won. A fourth man had no cloak, and his armor was close-meshed mail, his sword barely half the length of the others. But he looked every bit as much the warrior as the first three.

"Do you know them?" Kral asked.

"I know one," Donial said. "The one on the left, there. That's Rufio, one of Uncle's Rangers. The others I have never seen. They look like mercenaries to me."

"Is it not possible that your father's staff hired some mercenaries in your absence, to help guard his house?"

"It is possible," Alanya admitted. "But not likely. And anyway, since Rufio is with them, that must mean that Uncle Lupinius is inside. First he took our father's life and everything of value we own, and now he has taken father's house as well."

Kral drew his knife from its scabbard. "Then we shall get it back," he said. "And the Teeth with it."

Alanya reached over unsteadily from her mount and restrained him. "The three of us, exhausted from the road, against those four? We wouldn't have a chance."

"There is always a chance, as long as blood runs in the veins of a warrior," Kral said.

"You are a warrior," Alanya pointed out. "But Donial is barely more than a boy—"

"I can fight!" Donial interjected.

"—and I have never lifted a weapon in battle," she continued. "Even if you could slay three of them, the fourth would surely kill you, Kral. And then where would we be?"

"But, if we know that he dwells therein—"

"If we know he's inside," Alanya interrupted, "then we can assume he's here for a while. We can study the situation, come up with a better plan than just blindly attacking a well-guarded gate."

The truth of her words gnawed at Kral. He knew she was right; he had utilized the same strategy when harassing the settlers' wall, back home. He hadn't been foolish enough just to charge them at their most fortified point. He had watched, learned their weak points, formulated an attack based on the information he acquired. He was not stronger than the entire army at Koronaka, so he had to be smarter. The same applied here.

At any rate, he could afford to wait a day or two. If he couldn't find a way in during that time, then he could go back to the idea of simply approaching the guards and killing as many as he could.

"What now?" Donial asked. "We cannot go in. If Lupinius knew we had followed him here from Koronaka, he would probably have us killed, or at least thrown into a dungeon somewhere."

"Father's home has no dungeons," Alanya reminded him. "I agree, we dare not go inside." She backed her horse away from the square, and Donial and Kral followed suit, lest the guards see them and recognize the siblings. She pondered for a few moments, then Kral saw her light up. "I know. Cheveray!"

"Yes!" Donial said, evidently with enthusiastic agreement.

"Who?" Kral asked.

"Cheveray," Alanya said again. "Father's best friend, solicitor, business partner. He's practically an uncle to us—more so than Lupinius ever was, for that matter. He was supposed to take care of Father's affairs here while Father was on his mission for the king. If Lupinius has moved into the house, he will know about it—and he will know how to get him out."

They turned their mounts and started off at a steady walk for the home of this Cheveray. Kral was suddenly uneasy. He had imagined coming into the city and staying in a house with Alanya and Donial—a house that was otherwise unoccupied. He had not really given much thought to the fact that he might have to interact with other Aquilonians, beyond agreeing to wear Donial's clothes, to help hide the fact of his race. He knew all too well that Picts and Aquilonians were natural enemies. Would this Cheveray accept him as a friend of his friend's children? Or would he summon the Aquilonian armies and have Kral killed or imprisoned? His gut tensed, and he realized he was riding more stiffly, less comfortably, than he had before.

He would not want to have come this far only to be betrayed by the person Alanya and Donial trusted most in all of Tarantia.

22

LUPINIUS ENJOYED THE luxury of his brother's home. The bedding was of silks and satins, the pillows plush and soft, the tapestries on the walls heavy and rich, the marble floors smooth. Invictus's cook, an elderly woman named Arigan, had fed him a delectable lamb stew with fresh vegetables she had bought in Tarantia's markets that very day. His brother had a fine collection of wines and ales, which Lupinius was not shy about sampling.

All in all, he felt, he had made the right choice in coming here. He could happily live in this house for the rest of his life, enjoying the fruits of his brother's labors.

But he knew that he couldn't coast forever on the goodwill people felt for Invictus. There would come a time when even Arigan would want some gold to cross her palm. The mercenaries he had hired in the square that day, to replace the Rangers killed by the brigands' ambush, would want to be paid sooner than that.

Lupinius had a nice place to live, but little enough left with which to support that life. He needed to do something soon. If he was not to sell the household furnishings, he would have to go back to his original plan. He had carried that ugly crown all this way, even when his own skin was at risk. His first step would be to find out what it really was. Powerful magics brought high prices. Selling that, and maybe his niece's bejeweled mirror, should hold him for a while.

Lupinius had had occasion, in the past, to make the acquaintance of a magician named Kanilla Rey. This mage had never become too ambitious for his own good, never allowed his thirst for knowledge and power to lead him down those dark and often deadly paths that some took. He seemed content to sell his services from time to time, and to study his books, practice his spells, and live a life of relative peace and comfort here in Tarantia.

Lupinius had one of Invictus's household servants, a dour but muscular Kothian, carry the crown in its wooden box to Kanilla Rey's home. Standing in the street with the Kothian just behind and two trusted Rangers standing guard, he rapped upon Kanilla Rey's door. Several minutes passed, then the magician himself opened it.

"Lupinius?" he said. His skin was as dark as a Stygian's, and his hair as black, but his features were broad and open, almost jovial. Lupinius had never been able to figure out his origins. The mage blinked several times, as if he had been asleep or concentrating fiercely over something. "I had thought you somewhere in the wilderness, lording it over the locals."

"And so I was," Lupinius agreed. "But then I came across something strange and wondrous, and I thought, who but my friend Kanilla Rey would want to see this? So here I am."

Kanilla Rey's smile was hesitant. He knew that to characterize their acquaintance as a friendship was an exaggeration, and that therefore Lupinius must want something. But Lupinius knew, also, that his curiosity would get the better of him. He would ignore the fact that he was being played.

The magician was heavy, probably twice Lupinius's weight. Lupinius had never been sure if his bulk was fat or muscle. He was barrel-chested, and his gut was as round and firm as a drum. His arms and legs were perpetually swathed in fine yellow linens. On his body he wore a short robe of purple satin with gilt filigree running through it. Lupinius thought the yellow looked comical, sticking out from beneath that robe. But he had dressed that way as long as Lupinius had known him, so it suited him in some fashion.

"Come in, then," Kanilla Rey said, stepping back to make room in the doorway for his visitors. He scratched his bare head, mussing his thick black hair. "There's a table in here on which your man can put that box."

Lupinius indicated that the Rangers should wait outside and bade the Kothian enter. The man set the box on the table Kanilla Rey had indicated. After he had put it down, he stood with his hands clasped behind his back until Lupinius dismissed him. When the man had gone, Kanilla Rey closed the door, turning back to Lupinius and the mysterious box. "So, my friend," he said, rubbing his hands together as he regarded the container. "What have you brought into my house?"

Lupinius hesitated for a moment. He and Kanilla Rey were far from friends, although both had used that word in the last few minutes. They had met several years past, before Lupinius had left for the borderland to seek his fortune. Lupinius had had occasion to require the services of a sorcerer who wouldn't ask many questions and would keep his mouth shut. The matter had been one of romance, and Kanilla Rey's efforts had proven successful.

He had trusted the man then, and his trust had not been betrayed. He had no choice but to do it again. Without Kanilla Rey's expertise he might never know just what the crown he had found really was, what powers it might wield.

Without speaking, he went to the box and unlatched it. Lamplight from the wall sconces shone into the open lid, illuminating the bone-and-tooth headpiece within. Kanilla Rey glanced at Lupinius, then leaned over the box, looking in with a blank expression.

After a moment, he reached into the box. "May I remove it?" he asked.

"By all means," Lupinius answered. "Have a care, though—I fear it is fragile."

"Of course," Kanilla Rey assured him. He pulled the crown from its resting place and held it toward the light, turning it gently in his hands. He perused it from every angle. "Interesting," he said softly. "Very interesting."

"Have you ever seen its like?" Lupinius asked anxiously.

"Not exactly," Kanilla Rey hedged. He shared that, at least, with his magical brethren, Lupinius recalled. None of them could ever give a straight answer to a question.

"Have you any idea what it is?" Lupinius pressed. "I had it from a Pictish shaman, who swore to its value." He didn't mind lying to the sorcerer, but still trusted that the sorcerer would be honest with him, as he would be paying in gold for Kanilla Rey's expertise and time. He didn't want to tell how fiercely the Picts had fought to protect it, or that magic had played a role in its defense. If he did, the magician would surely try to cheat him out of it.

Kanilla Rey shrugged. "At a glance, I would say that it's simply a relic, of value only for its antiquity, and probably only to another Pict. I'll do a little research to see if I can learn more about it. But it is simply bones and teeth, with no mystical significance that I can detect. It is some barbarian's idea of good taste, nothing more. If you'd like, I can dispose of it for you here."

Lupinius didn't even consider the magician's offer. If it was worth doing further research on, then it was worth holding on to. Even if Kanilla Rey's first impression was correct, someone would probably part with a couple of gold coins for it, just as a curiosity. There were those in Tarantia who collected primitive objects to display in their homes. But this, he knew, was more than a simple curiosity. "No, I'll take it back with me," he said, determined to understate his case. "If nothing else, it will amuse me to keep it around the house. But if you learn any more about it, please let me know."

"Of course," Kanilla Rey promised. He watched in disinterested silence as Lupinius closed up the box, then summoned the Kothian to carry it home. The two men shared some meaningless pleasantries, and Lupinius left Kanilla Rey to his studies.

KANILLA REY WAITED for thirty minutes after Lupinius left, in case the man returned for any reason. When he didn't, the magician went deeper into his home, into his private sanctum sanctorum, where he kept his magical supplies: the potions, tools, and implements he needed for his spells. This room was always kept discreetly illuminated by a pair of glowing stones that rested on tall columns. They filled the room with a soft, greenish light.

He didn't hesitate, but went straight to yet another stone, a chipped and craggy boulder that rested permanently on the floor near the center of the crowded space. Drawing a small, sharp knife from beneath the folds of his robes, he sliced open his finger and allowed seven drops of blood to drip onto the stone's surface. When the blood hit the rock, it sizzled as if falling onto hot coals. The room was filled with the aroma of rose petals. Kanilla Rey inhaled the scent and spoke some words of power. *"Ia nimtu kenata ia ia!"*

As he said them, the surface of the rock visibly altered. The gray crust seemed to melt away, and the rock took on the clarity of clean, pure water. Kanilla Rey stared into the now-transparent rock, as if seeing something there that no one else could. As he did, he spoke again. *"Quietus nictu camala Shehkmi al Nasir,"* he said, repeating the same phrase a dozen times. By the tenth, the rock had begun to grow cloudy. By the twelfth, it had cleared again, only now there was an image of a man's head, so distinct it was as if the man was right there in the room.

Shehkmi al Nasir glared at him across the miles, with thinly veiled malice putting fire in his dark eyes. The Stygian sorcerer had a narrow, hooded face that reminded Kanilla Rey of a vulture's just after a satisfying meal. The skin of his head was hairless, the usual dusky shade of the Stygians, but marked by a latticework of scars. Kanilla Rey had never known if these indicated a youth of battle or some sort of ritual scarification. His earlobes had been cut away, and lines of black dots, tattooed at some point, descended from beneath his eyes, down his cheeks to his jawline. When he smiled, Kanilla Rey involuntarily shuddered; it was like watching a snake tell a joke.

"It has been a long time, Kanilla Rey," he said. His voice was only slightly muffled, though he was thousands of miles from this spot. "Why have you summoned me today?"

"I have seen a strange object today," Kanilla Rey told him. "I hoped to utilize your vast resource of knowledge, to see what you may be able to tell me about it."

"What was it?" Shehkmi al Nasir asked him.

"A Pictish crown of some sort," Kanilla Rey described. "Made of bones, joined together with fine copper, and decorated with large teeth. They looked like the teeth of a bear, though bigger than any bear's I have ever seen."

"A bone crown," Shehkmi al Nasir mused. "How old would you guess it was?"

"Old," Kanilla Rey answered without pause. "The bones are browned with age, though the teeth retain their whiteness."

"Do you have possession of this crown?"

"No," Kanilla Rey admitted. "Though I know where I can get it."

"I recommend that you do so," the Stygian said. "I cannot say with any certainty that the thing is worth any trouble or expense at all. But it might be. I would have to see it to know for sure. If you have the opportunity to take possession of it and deliver it here to me, I will be able to make more informed speculation."

Kanilla Rey was heartened by this report. Shehkmi al Nasir was no doubt holding back information, as he was himself. He hadn't told the Stygian, for example, that when he held the crown in his own hands he felt a distinct thrum of supernatural power emanating from within. At a glance, the thing had looked worthless, but when he'd held it he had known that it was a magical object of considerable potency. If he had told Shehkmi al Nasir about that, however, the sorcerer would certainly have tried to cheat him and take the crown for himself. He wanted information that he could use to determine how hard he should try to get the thing, but he was not interested in losing it to a rival magician. He and Shehkmi al Nasir had been allies many times. But in the circles of magicians, a friend today could become an enemy tomorrow, if enough was at stake.

He had felt, upon first touching the crown, that it was something he wanted to have. Shehkmi al Nasir's interest in it—unstated though it was—merely confirmed that. If he had known earlier that his sometime friend would be so curious about it, he would have killed Lupinius on the spot and simply taken it. The Rangers would have objected, but he could have dealt with them.

Waiting was only a minor inconvenience. He would still have it. It would just take a while longer. He bade the Stygian farewell and retired to another room to lay his plans.

23

CHEVERAY PROVED EVERY bit as pleasant and generous as Alanya remembered. He was an older man, old enough to be her father's father, and he walked stooped over, with the aid of a cane. In spite of his infirmity, he was full of manic energy and unquenchable mirth. When Alanya and Donial had shown up last night, with Kral in tow, he had thrown the door wide and enveloped the three of them, Pict included, in a bone-crushing hug.

"Children!" he shouted, beaming. "It's so good to see you! Come in, come in!"

They had done so, and Cheveray had insisted that they spend most of the night telling him about everything they had done in the border region, while they ate food he had servants bring in. He had heard about Invictus's death, had mourned for the traditional week, and expressed profound grief to his friend's children. Finally, he had servants make up separate rooms for each of them and insisted that they stay in his house as long as they were in the city.

Alanya slept like the dead.

The sun was already sinking into the west when one of Cheveray's servants, a mute Hyrkanian woman, roused her. Using gestures, she made Alanya understand that the others were already up and waiting for her in Cheveray's dining room. Alanya dressed quickly and joined them.

A feast of meats, breads, and fruits waited on Cheveray's big table. Kral had cleared several plates, from the looks of things, and Donial was busily putting away his share. Cheveray sipped a hot beverage and watched them, gracing Alanya with a broad smile when she entered.

"Welcome, Alanya," he said. He was thin and short—a trait exaggerated by his stoop. His hair was white and shoulder length, his features oddly large for a man of such diminutive stature. "Sit, eat. You must be famished after your journey."

"I am a bit hungry," Alanya admitted, starting toward an empty chair.

Before she was even seated, Cheveray spoke again. "I have some interesting information," he said. "You are right that your uncle has moved into your father's house. I made no protest, as I had no knowledge that the two of you yet lived. From what I hear, he has terrorized the staff into staying on. One tried to protest and was immediately butchered by Lupinius's soldiers. The rest have been cowed into submission."

Alanya felt her cheeks burn at the idea. Father's household staff had been with him for years, had practically raised her and Donial from childhood. "That's terrible!"

"Yes, it is," Cheveray agreed sympathetically. "I will get word to the rest, when I can do so discreetly, that they can seek sanctuary here, and I will protect them. But more urgently, I have some sense now of what Lupinius's goal is here in Tarantia."

"He has a goal, beyond just using our father's wealth as his own?" Donial asked.

"He seems to," Cheveray replied. "He has been sending

feelers out into the city, to see if anyone is interested in purchasing some kind of relic. The way I hear it described, it's a strange, toothed crown."

Alanya turned to Kral, whose jaw hung open. "The Teeth!" he shouted.

"So it would seem," Alanya said. "We thought he had it. Now we know for sure. And I'm certain he has my mirror, as well."

During their late-hours talk, Kral had mentioned the Teeth of the Ice Bear to Cheveray. Alanya had meant to bring up the mirror, but the conversation had shifted, and in her weariness she had forgotten to mention it. Now, Cheveray turned toward her. "Which mirror?"

"My mother's," she said. "It's jeweled on the back, with a lovely carved handle."

A darkness seemed to cloud Cheveray's usually chipper face. "I was afraid you would say that," he said.

"You know the mirror?"

"Of course," Cheveray replied. "It was very important to both of your parents. I never did know much about it, just that they kept it close, and that it's a magical object of some kind."

"Are you sure?" Her father had hinted at that from time to time, but she had always assumed he was joking.

"Your father did not just keep it because it was a memento of your mother," Cheveray said. "He kept it because of its powers—powers he wanted you and your brother to have when you reached maturity."

"I'm mature!" Donial insisted.

Cheveray smiled and nodded. "Yes, you are. I should have said when you reach full adulthood, as Alanya almost has. Now that both your parents are gone, girl, you are the adult of the family. That mirror belongs to you, by all rights. As does the house. I will get word to the king that Lupinius is here, in the city. Judging by your story, I would not be surprised if he was anxious to meet your uncle. At least, he would be if he heard your version of it. He sought only peace with the Picts."

Alanya nodded. She would be happy to explain things to King Conan, if the opportunity presented itself.

But the mirror loomed even larger in her thoughts. She couldn't have said why, but she had always suspected there was more to that mirror than her father had told her. Not just an icon with which to remember and honor her parents, but something much more—a kind of birthright that she had yet to discover fully. She sympathized with Kral's search for his people's crown, but he didn't even really know why he was chasing it. To him it was a symbol of something he couldn't truly grasp.

The mirror had always been important to her, on a deeply personal level, connecting her to the mother she missed so much—and now to her father as well. Beyond that, it had value on a monetary level. Thanks to Cheveray, she understood that it was still more than all that. Her parents had meant for her to have it, and presumably for the mirror—either through its value, its magical properties, or both—to protect and provide for their family when they no longer could.

Their uncle had betrayed them in so many ways. Somehow, he was responsible for the murder of their father. He had stolen from them. He had taken over their father's house, which was rightfully theirs. Which was, in fact, the only place on earth that was truly home.

He was blood, family, and that would have meant something once.

No longer.

"We need to go there," she insisted. "We need to get that mirror back before he sells it, too."

"And the Teeth," Kral reminded her.

"Of course," Alanya agreed, although now that was secondary, as far as she was concerned.

"I shall gather some men," Cheveray said. "I am no

longer young enough to fight myself, Mitra knows. Not
that I was ever much good in a fray, with this back. But I
have enough wealth to hire a band of mercenaries sufficient to storm Invictus's estate."

Kral waved his hand dismissively. "There is no time for
that," he said. "If Lupinius is already trying to sell the
Teeth, it could be gone at any moment. Then we would be
right back where we started, trying to determine its where-
abouts. No, I'll go in tonight."

"Impossible!" Cheveray declared.

Alanya smiled slyly. "You do not know Kral," she said.
"If anyone can do it, he can."

"I can," Kral confirmed. "And I will."

"But not alone," Alanya reminded him.

"I have to go alone," he protested. "It's the only way I
can—"

"I will go with you," Alanya said. "You do not know the
first thing about the house or grounds. I know it well, and I
know the staff, in case we need assistance. Besides, the
mirror is mine, and the house should be as well."

Kral shot her an odd expression, as if he couldn't decide
whether to be annoyed or impressed. *Probably he can't,*
she thought. He looked like he was about to respond when
Donial cut in.

"I'm going, too!" he insisted.

Cheveray's lean face was turning red as he listened.
Finally, he sputtered, "Children, I am not going to
allow—"

"Donial and I have the deepest respect and love for you,
Cheveray," Alanya interrupted. "But you are not our parents, and we must make our own decisions about this. Besides, I am no child—you yourself said I was the woman of
the family now."

Cheveray's jaw worked for a moment, as if he weren't
finished, but finally he nodded. "I did indeed," he admitted.
"I must still make my displeasure known—you are both

too young and inexperienced for something like this, even if Kral is not."

"I agree," Kral said.

"Perhaps," Alanya agreed. "But I'm going along just the same. I will not speak for Donial, but that home is his birthright as well, and if he wants to come, I say we let him."

"I *am* coming," Donial said. "I will not stay behind, so you're better off letting me stay with you."

"He is right about that," Alanya pointed out. "If he tries to get in by himself, he's likely to raise an alarm that will get us all caught."

Kral had apparently made up his mind. "You can both come with me," he said. "But you follow my instructions. You go where I say, do what I say, immediately and without argument. Can you agree to that?"

"Of course," Alanya said.

Donial's reply took a moment longer, but he agreed as well.

"Good," Kral said, when both had promised to obey him. He suggested they take twenty minutes to prepare, then be ready to leave. As Alanya went to her room to get ready, she felt a knot of anxiety in her stomach. But it was leavened with excitement, and even a little relief. They would get the Teeth, and the mirror, tonight, or die in the effort.

LUPINIUS WAITED IN the den of his brother's home, with the crown in its box on a wide, finely carved table. He had received a message from a man named Declariat, who had expressed an interest in the barbaric curiosity. Lupinius had let a select few people know he had something of that nature available for sale, and one of them—a man who dealt in stolen goods, often as not—had told this Declariat, a well-known collector of such things, about it.

Lupinius had inquired about Declariat and learned that he was a wealthy man who enjoyed mystical objects, with little concern about how they had been acquired.

Hoping for a healthy profit for his efforts, Lupinius put great effort into looking as if he was casual about trying to unload the crown, without actually needing the money he might receive. So he had put on some of his brother's finest clothing, and he waited in the well-appointed den with only a single Ranger, Rufio, on guard in the outer room. A butterlamp burned on the table near the box, as Declariat had insisted on meeting at night. Lupinius waited, sipping Hyrkanian wine and trying to be patient, until finally he heard a sound from the outer room.

He had arrived, then. Good.

Lupinius cleared his throat, and at a soft tapping on the door, said, "Enter."

He kept his seat behind the table as Declariat came in. The man was younger than he had expected, but dressed in a noble's finery: loose blue silks with fine gold filigree, matching tights, and a feathered cap that drooped over his left eye. He was lean and tall, almost sticklike. Lupinius felt he had made the right move by keeping only one Ranger standing guard—this man wouldn't frighten a child.

"You are Declariat?" he asked.

"Indeed," the man said. He touched his hat in salute. "Greetings."

"Some wine?" Lupinius offered, waving toward the cask that stood beside him.

"Thanks, but I prefer to get right to business," Declariat said. "You have an interesting object, I'm told."

"A curiosity," Lupinius agreed. He played a curious kind of juggling game, talking down the crown's attributes to Kanilla Rey, and enhancing them to this potential buyer. "Very rare, they say, and possessing incredible powers. One of a kind."

"So I hear," Declariat said. He jingled a purse hidden beneath the folds of his tunic. "Just the kind of thing I am interested in. May I see it?"

Encouraged by the sound of gold coins, Lupinius stood and opened the box for the visitor. He took the crown from the box and set it gingerly on the table. If this worked, his brother owned many other art objects he might be able to sell, to keep income flowing his way for some time. "Here it is," he said. "A true Pictish treasure."

Declariat's voice was hushed when he spoke again. "Very nice," he said. "Condition is very good. And you're right, it is a rarity. I have never seen one quite like it. Do you know its age or origin?"

"I have not been able to find out," Lupinius replied. "That's how rare it is."

Declariat lifted it carefully and turned it under the light of the lamp. "I am impressed," he said. "Very."

"If you would like to add it to your collection," Lupinius said, "just state your offer."

Declariat grinned wolfishly. "How about if I just help myself to it?"

Lupinius's hand dropped to the knife at his belt. "You wouldn't dare! Surely you saw the guard outside this door."

"He will not interfere," Declariat said simply.

Lupinius felt his gut tighten. He slipped out from behind the table, drawing his knife and, giving Declariat a wide berth, crossed to the door. Flinging it open, he saw that Rufio was slumped to the floor, blood pooling around him.

This twig of a man had murdered one of his sturdiest Rangers, while Lupinius sat only a few feet away!

"There are plenty more—" he began.

"Drinking, in your dining hall. Over their merriment, they will hear nothing. Just save yourself any trouble and let me leave with it."

"Never!" Lupinius charged the little man, but his opponent was as quick as he was slender. Before Lupinius reached him, he had dodged to one side and drawn a sliver-thin rapier from some hiding place. Lupinius halted his charge and backed away, knowing that with his sword, Declariat's reach was much greater than his own.

"You are not Declariat at all, are you?" he asked, suddenly realizing how he had been tricked. His contact had no doubt simply told one of his regular criminal suppliers to impersonate the collector in order to get his own hands on the crown.

"No," the imposter answered. He feinted right with the rapier, and Lupinius raised his knife, dodging left at the same time. Another feint, another dodge. Sweat broke out on Lupinius's temples, his upper lip. The man was *playing* him.

"Guards!" he screamed. The man had been bluffing about so much else, maybe he was about that as well.

Barely had the word escaped his lips than the false Declariat lunged at him, though, the rapier's blade whipping the air toward him. Lupinius lurched backward but the blade's tip caught the loose fabric of his robe and tore it. He took another step back, and felt solid wall behind him.

The man's blade whistled as he sliced the air with it, weaving a shimmering pattern in the lamplight. Lupinius realized he had one decent chance to survive: If he could get into the outer room, and get his hands on Rufio's sword, he could beat this opponent.

One chance. He reached behind himself and tugged down a velvet wall hanging, which he hurled toward the other man. As soon as he had thrown it, he dashed for the door.

But the imposter was faster.

Avoiding the tapestry, he raced toward the door and turned, sword extended. Lupinius saw its narrow length too late to dodge. His feet slid on the marble floor as he tried to backpedal. The blade bit into his chest, and he felt a hot, piercing pain. He let out a gurgling cry and dropped to his knees, and the man who had called himself Declariat withdrew his blade.

He looked almost sadly at Lupinius. "I offered you the choice," he said sympathetically.

Lupinius tried to respond, but his voice no longer obeyed him. He suddenly felt cold. His legs gave way completely, dumping him to the floor. He clawed at the marble with one hand, still hoping to summon aid, or to stop the thief one way or another. But the floor was growing dark, and everything was suddenly so quiet.

So quiet . . .

24

KRAL WAS FRUSTRATED.

The city was so vast—block after block of buildings, all surrounded by walls, and outside those, cultivated fields—that it seemed there was no forest left in the world.

Without forest, he couldn't find the berries he needed to crush to make his blue war paint. He didn't need the paint to fight, he was sure—just as he had learned he didn't need the presence of his clansmen, or the wild war cries, or to let the battle frenzy sweep him up. But he knew it helped to disguise him, helped him blend into the shadows of night.

Traditions, he believed, had their origins in utility. Certainly that one did.

Without the right berries, he resorted to going out into the streets and finding mud he could smear on his body. He would go into battle as he always did, naked but for his loincloth. With the mud streaking his face, torso, and limbs, he would be nearly invisible in the dark.

He had suggested to Alanya and Donial that they do the same. Neither was comfortable fighting nearly naked,

however. They settled on dark tunics and leggings. Each
carried a knife and a short sword, provided by Cheveray.
He wasn't sure Alanya would know what to do with one,
and Donial's expertise seemed to exist mostly in his own
mind. With luck they wouldn't need them at all. But if it
came to trouble, better they be armed than not.

Both showed up in front of Cheveray's house, in less
time than the twenty minutes he had allowed. Both were
quiet, almost solemn. Nervous, he guessed. He had infil-
trated the wall at Koronaka enough times to become accustomed to it. While it wasn't a casual thing, at least he knew
what to expect. Neither Alanya or Donial had ever done
anything like this.

One good thing about the city was that its warren of
buildings offered plenty of shadow. Light spilled from occasional windows and doors, but those could generally be
avoided, and even when not, they were not so large that it
took much time to pass through them. They went on foot,
rather than mounted, as it was easier to stay out of sight.

He thought all was lost at one point. Ahead, a large
group of people clotted a street corner they needed to
cross. With a wave, Kral halted their progress, and they
pressed back against the dark buildings. He nodded them
back the way they had come. They went around the far corner, down to the next cross street.

But it was the same there—a large clutch of people
standing on the corner, looking at something in the street.
"What is it, a parade?" Donial whispered.

"I know not," Kral said quietly. "But they block our
path."

"Let's have a closer look," Alanya suggested. "Maybe
we can tell how long it will take."

Kral wasn't happy about that idea, but it was her city.
If she thought the street might clear momentarily, that
would be better than having to detour around whatever
this was. Cautiously, they approached the corner. The fact

that everyone there was looking into the street made it easier to remain unobserved.

It took only a minute to see that the people weren't
gathered to watch a parade, but a king.

It must have been hard, Kral thought, for the king to
travel anywhere within his city without attracting a mob of
spectators. For him, the option of simply stepping away
from his throne didn't exist. There were always people
around him—advisors, servants, people who wanted to
draw his attention to one issue or another. Even in the Bear
Clan village, the chief found it hard to achieve solitude,
and there were thousands more people in the city than
there.

And if that had not been a problem, there was still another. Kral had never seen a king before, much less one as
important and exalted as King Conan of Aquilonia. But the
sight almost took his breath away. He knew, looking upon
King Conan, what the word "majestic" meant, though he
didn't know how to say it in Aquilonian.

The king was tall in the saddle. His armor was golden,
shining even in the dim light of the street, with a scarlet
cloak draped behind him. His arms were massive, as were
the thighs that gripped his saddle. His hair was black as
night, cut squarely across his forehead. His eyes were as
blue as clear water, and shone with evident intelligence.
His mouth turned up in a slight smile as he regarded his
subjects—now waving to women in a tavern's doorway,
now calling out to a man by name, now nodding to the
crowd on a corner.

"King Conan!" voices shouted. Kral had the sensation
that people just wanted to be noticed by him, just to feel
that he had acknowledged their existence. "King Conan!"

Almost caught up in the moment, Kral had to fight
down the urge to add his own shout to the din. He glanced
back at Alanya and Donial. Both beamed up at the king as
he rode past them. Alanya had a nearly beatific smile on

her face, her eyes wide and moist. Donial's jaw had
dropped open, and his right fist was tight on the grip of his
sword, as if ready to fight for his king at the Cimmerian's
slightest request.

The three of them stood there, silently, as the king receded from view down the street. When he was past, the
knots of people on the corners broke up. People wandered
away, most chatting excitedly about what they had just seen.
Conan seemed universally popular, at least among these
people—working people, Kral could tell, not nobility.

It only took a matter of minutes before the streets were
clear, once the king and his retinue had passed. Kral,
Alanya, and Donial simply waited until most people had
gone about their own business, then they crossed over and
made their way toward Lupinius and the Teeth.

GORIAN HAD SERVED Kanilla Rey many times over
the years. He never remembered what he did for the magician, but he was always paid for his services—extra if he
had been wounded in the doing of whatever task Kanilla
Rey had set out for him. He knew that sometimes he was
sent to do dangerous things, and he was usually partnered
with men he had never seen before and would never see
again. These were some of the ways Kanilla Rey protected
his own interests. That was fine with Gorian. He always
knew what he was about when the job needed to be done. It
was only after that his memory was altered in some way.

Tonight he and three others had been sent to a house
with which he was vaguely familiar—that of Invictus, an
ambassador of the king. He had been assured that Invictus
was dead and that someone else was staying in the house.
That someone else, a man named Lupinius, had an object,
a crown of bones and teeth, that Kanilla Rey wanted. There
would be soldiers guarding it, but Gorian and his fellows
were ready for that.

Gorian glanced around at the men he was to work with—tough men, warriors who carried the scars of combat upon their flesh. None of them knew one another's name. Gorian knew only from appearances and accents that he walked with a Turanian, a Gunderman, and a Zamoran. He knew nothing beyond that about them and didn't want to. From time to time he had thought it might prove worthwhile to write down what he knew of the missions Kanilla Rey sent him on, while he still remembered. But Gorian could neither read nor write. At any rate, to cross Kanilla Rey probably meant to invite certain death.

Approaching the house of Invictus, Gorian saw that soldiers did indeed guard the house. There were only two at the gate, however. From their flushed faces and unsteady legs, he suspected that they had been drinking.

"Easy," the Zamoran said. He was a blocky man with a thick shock of dark hair and eyes like a bottomless well. "I'll take them."

Gorian, nominally in charge of the group, nodded his assent. The Zamoran affected a drunken stagger. As he neared the guards, they laughed at him instead of attempting an alert response. When they came toward him, either to help him or to mock him further, he straightened suddenly. With practiced efficiency, he drove his knife into one's breast, then across the other's throat. With barely a sound and only seconds lost, both guards fell to the ground.

Gorian and the other two hurried across to the gate, which the Zamoran was already opening for them. Inside the compound were several buildings. The main house was two stories tall, stately columns and sturdy walls gleaming whitely in the moonlight. Nearby, a lower building likely served as servants' quarters and possibly barracks for guards. Fragrant woodsmoke and loud laughter drifted from another, which Gorian took to be a dining and drinking hall. A couple were obviously storage buildings, yet another a stable. The buildings were arranged around a large central square, flagstoned and planted with trees and flower beds. It might have been a pleasant environment, a refuge from busy city streets, a place for relaxation and meditation, but the flowers had been trampled, and trash littered the open square.

Gorian had no interest in any of these things. The faster he and his comrades found the crown and delivered it into the hands of Kanilla Rey, the faster he would be paid. Kanilla Rey would perform whatever magic it was that made him forget his task—he couldn't even remember how the wizard did that—but he would have gold in his purse.

All these separate buildings could make the search more complicated, but Kanilla Rey had insisted that the crown would be close to Lupinius. And Lupinius, as the new master of the property, would be in the main house.

The grounds were quiet, except for the noise coming from the presumed dining hall. Gorian pointed to it, so that his fellows would understand to keep away from it, then he pointed his head toward the main house. "In there," he muttered. The others nodded their agreement. Keeping an eye on that building in case anyone ventured forth, Gorian and the others hurried across the open square toward the main house. Lamps burned through some of the windows, but no one appeared to be present.

The front door was ajar. Gorian opened it slowly, peering inside. He saw no one. The front room was marble-floored, with a couple of tables bearing statuary and tapestries decorating the walls. Doors led away from the room in both directions. Gorian slipped inside, his sword drawn.

At the door to the next room, he looked inside and saw a corpse.

Silently, he gestured for the others to join him. Pointing toward the body, slumped in a pool of blood, he whispered, "Stay alert!"

They walked through a room that seemed to be a sitting room, barely disturbing the fat flies gorging themselves on fresh gore. The man looked like a soldier, armored and armed, but nearly decapitated by a savage attack. Light flickered through the open doorway on the other side of the room. Gorian headed for that, taking in sharp, shallow breaths of air. The shifting shadows in there made him more on edge than ever, lest he be taken by surprise by the presence of someone more alive than the fallen soldier.

He looked around once more at his companions, reassuring himself that they were all ready for whatever might come. When he had done so, he cautiously approached the doorway to the next room. He risked a glance inside.

Another corpse met his gaze there.

Otherwise, the room was deserted. He went in, blowing out the breath he had been holding, and looked at this body. Another man, this one clad in the garb of a wealthy man. He had fallen forward into a wide pool of blood.

On a table, a lamp burned next to a cask of wine and a wooden box. Gorian went to the box and looked into its shadowed depths. Empty.

Just in case, he reached in and felt around the box's interior. His hand brushed something hard and dry and jagged, closed on it. He brought it out, into the lamplight.

A single tooth. Larger than any he had ever seen, but still unmistakable.

Gorian was uneducated and of questionable morals, but he was not a stupid man. It only took him a second to figure out what had happened. He had been sent to fetch a crown made of bones and teeth. Two dead bodies—one a guard, one a wealthy man, a landowner—and an empty box containing a single tooth, added up to one thing. Someone had stolen the crown before he and his fellows had a chance to do the same.

"Damn!" he swore. "We've been beaten to the prize, men."

"Are you sure?" the Gunderman asked.

"Sure enough," Gorian answered. He pointed toward the body on the ground. "That's Lupinius, master of the house,

I'd wager. And this tooth shows that the crown had been kept in this box. It's empty now, and the man's dead, as is the guard outside. If we don't want to be accused of these crimes, we'd best get on our way now."

"Agreed," the Turanian put in.

"Let's go," added the Zamoran.

Just as carefully as they had entered, they left the house and grounds. Gorian did not look forward to confessing their failure to Kanilla Rey. Better to get it over with, though. If he knew of it before they arrived, he would be twice as angry as if they told him themselves.

25

DONIAL WAS STILL reeling a little from the glimpse of King Conan, looking powerful and practically godlike in his armor and his majesty. He was the kind of ruler that a man could happily follow into battle, even into the very gates of hell if need be.

That was all put out of his mind as he watched strangers exit his father's property, passing the bodies of guards who either slept or had been killed. "Who are—?" he began.

Kral stifled his outburst. "Silence! Something is amiss. We need to figure out what."

"I have never seen those men," Alanya said. They stood in the shadows across the street from their childhood home. "But those guards look dead."

"I would suspect robbery," Kral added. "Except if they have taken anything, it is only something small enough to hide on their persons. None of them carries anything large enough to be the crown."

"How do we get in, then?" Donial asked. He had wanted to turn Kral over to Aquilonian authorities, when they started their journey. But along the way, that had changed. He would never forgive the Picts for the death of his father—but he was no longer certain that they carried the blame. He mistrusted them on principle, but Kral seemed trustworthy. Donial was confused, and frightened. If he called out now, would he be treated any better than the Pict? "If someone sees those dead guards, then the alarm will be raised."

Kral led Donial and Alanya away from the gates, around the corner toward a section of the wall that stood unguarded. Here the three huddled together, away from the sounds of conversation. "Are there any other ways in?" Kral asked. "Or must we climb over the wall?"

"There is a smaller gate at the rear of the property, behind the stables," Alanya said. "No telling if it's guarded as well, but it was not, in my father's time. He had not as much to fear as Lupinius."

"We shall check that back gate, then," he said. "While darkness remains on our side."

"But . . . even if we get in the gate," Donial pointed out, "the place will be crawling with Rangers and the city guard. Someone besides us will see those bodies soon."

"I slipped in and out of Koronaka, and across the wall, while it was guarded by some of those same Rangers, and more," Kral said. "Why should this be any more difficult?"

"Besides," Alanya added, "we know the grounds better than anyone, Donial. Come, this needs doing, and now is the time."

Donial nodded, reluctant but unwilling to abandon his sister. That mirror meant more to Alanya than it did to him, but his sister's happiness was important, so he would go wherever she led. The three of them rounded the next corner, which took them into an alley behind the compound.

Across the alley, blank walls marked off the property of another noble, one wealthier by far than their father. The front gate of that complex was on the opposite wall, so it was unlikely that anyone would see them as they approached their own back gate.

As it turned out, the back gate was indeed unguarded. In fact, it hung open. "Hardly anyone ever used this entrance," Alanya explained. "I used to, sometimes, if I wanted to get away from the house without Father knowing."

The gate was narrow, just wide enough for one person at a time. Normally, it would have been closed and latched. Kral went through first, paused just inside, then motioned the others in after him. They were behind the stables here, and Donial could smell the horses inside, could hear them whickering nervously at the commotion elsewhere on the property. Raised voices and running footsteps drifted back from the front square.

At Kral's urging, they skirted the edge of the stables and headed toward the main house. Donial could see, near the corner, the window of the room that had been his bedroom for most of his life. The window was dark now, open to the elements, the glass broken from it. He felt a pang of regret, as if he had somehow been responsible for leaving the place unprotected.

Between the stable and the house was a short stretch of open ground, paved with flagstones, a continuation of the square in front. Garbage was strewn on the stones here: bottles, broken jars, and other refuse such as a group of military men might leave behind. There was a back door to the main house on that side, which Donial pointed out to Kral.

"If there are guards about they will be able to see the front door," Donial said. "So we should use this one."

Kral started for it, then suddenly took a step back, arms flung out, catching both Donial and Alanya and shoving them to the ground.

"Someone's coming!" he whispered hoarsely.

• • •

ALANYA BREATHED IN the scent of Kral—his anxious sweat, the mud he had smeared on his body—while he pressed her and Donial down against the flagstones. Pebbles ground into her back and hip, and Kral's weight, while not unpleasant, added to her immediate discomfort.

But he had been right. Though she had not heard them, two Rangers, one carrying a glowing lantern, came around the corner of the main house. Both had spears clutched in their free hands. ". . . good is being in the city if we spend all our time behind these walls?" one of them was saying. His words were slurred with drink.

The two Rangers didn't even glance into the shadows by the stable. As quickly as they had come, they were gone, around the far corner of the house. As their voices receded, Kral got up off Alanya and Donial.

"Sorry," he said.

"I didn't even hear them coming," Alanya admitted. "I'm glad you did."

"Living in this noisy city has no doubt ruined your ears," Kral speculated. "A Pict has to be able to hear the flap of a wing, the snap of a twig, the falling of a leaf. It's a matter of survival in the wilderness."

"We know all about your magnificent savage senses," Donial said, an edge of anger in his voice. "It's all you ever talk about."

"Donial!" Alanya scolded.

"Well, practically," Donial said.

"If it had not been for his senses, you would be in the hands of the Rangers right now," she pointed out.

Donial looked away and kicked at a loose stone. It clattered across the flagstones. Donial's hand went to his mouth, as if he had said something out loud. He looked up again, shamefaced. "I'm sorry."

"Just be careful," Alanya snapped. There must have

been something little brothers were good for, she thought, but she couldn't imagine what right at the moment.

They stayed in the shadows a minute longer, waiting and listening. Her heart was still hammering from the close call, but at least no one came to investigate the stone Donial had kicked.

When it seemed safe again, they crossed to the back door of the house. It was up several marble stairs, which they climbed quickly. This was an entrance used only by servants, and Alanya knew that it opened onto a small room that could be used as a staging area for dinners held in the home. Official functions, diplomatic affairs. Usually, she and Donial and Father ate in a small dining room here in the house, or even in the dining hall with the rest of the staff. But there was a grand ballroom in the house reserved for larger functions. This small room was where food was brought in to be served up for those gatherings.

It was dark when they went in, quiet. Only one other door led away from the room, into the grand ballroom. Alanya showed Kral where the door was. He opened it silently, just a crack. Enough to see through. Satisfied, he pulled it wider and stepped through.

Following, Alanya was mortified to see how the place had been mistreated. The huge, polished dining table was scarred, one of the chairs smashed to bits and others over-turned. Lupinius and his Rangers had only been living in the house for a few days, and yet it looked like a herd of oxen had trampled through. She stifled a gasp of shock.

Kral touched her arm, reminding her to remain silent. This room was empty, and it was evident at a glance that the mirror was not here. Alanya guessed that Lupinius would have kept it in his own bedroom, which would prob-ably be the same one that Father had used, upstairs. It was the largest and nicest of the bedrooms, with a view across the city and windows that could be opened on three sides to catch comforting breezes.

Several doors opened onto this room, and Kral looked at Alanya. "Which way?" he asked quietly.

Alanya shook her head, confused. Her uncle would probably be using Father's room as his own. But what was the meaning of the men they had seen leaving the property and the dead guards at the door?

There was no way to be sure without looking around. "Let's try upstairs," she whispered.

She proceeded to the door that would take them to the inner staircase. As Kral had done, she opened it only a little and held her eye close to the gap. She almost opened the door more, but then a flash of motion caught her eye, and she stopped herself. Arigan, a gray-haired woman in her fifties, and one of Father's most loyal retainers, rushed down the hallway carrying a bundle of something that Alanya couldn't make out. Alanya had always loved Arigan—the woman had been like a grandmother to her—and was tempted to call out to her.

But she held her tongue. There was no telling where Arigan's loyalties might lie now. Father no longer paid her. Since she had stayed on after Lupinius took over the property, she couldn't be trusted. Alanya waited until Arigan was well clear before venturing out into the hall and toward the stairs.

She climbed them, Kral and Donial both close at her heels. By the time she reached the top, she was out of breath. She knew it was because she was fighting back powerful emotions, here in her family's home.

They had almost gained the second floor when a door banged below them and a gruff voice shouted to someone outside. Alanya caught her breath and raced silently up the last two steps, then around a corner into the hallway. She didn't have time to check to make sure the hall was clear, but just wanted to get away from whoever was down below. Kral and Donial came right behind. Downstairs, the man continued down the hall they had just crossed and swept through another door.

"That was close," Donial breathed, after the man was gone.

"Too close," Kral agreed. "We must find the Teeth fast and get out of here."

"I thought you were the one who could do this easily," Donial said.

"Would you rather I started killing them?" Kral asked. "That would make it easier."

"No!" Alanya replied sharply. "That is not why we came."

"Not why *you* came," Kral said. "I would not hesitate."

"Kral . . ."

"I know, Alanya. Let's find your uncle."

Alanya nodded and led the way, passing by the door to her own room. She resisted the impulse to open it. If the Rangers had destroyed her things, she wasn't sure she could stand it. Maybe sometime later she would have the courage to look inside, but not just now.

Two rooms later, the door to her father's room was wide-open. She didn't hesitate but walked right in, ahead of Kral and Donial. Her sword was in her hand, though she hoped she wouldn't have to use it.

The room was vacant, but she could see at a glance that she was right about Lupinius having taken it as his own. Her father would never have left it in this condition, but Lupinius had never been as neat as he was. His clothing—and some of Father's, she recognized—was strewn across the bed and floor. Weapons lay in a messy tangle. Father had a chest in which he had kept those things most precious to him, and it was to it that Alanya went first. Scattered across the top of it were rings, bracelets, medallions and other pieces of jewelry that she recognized as belonging to Lupinius.

But mixed in with those things—half-buried under a coil of silver chain—she saw the handle of her mother's mirror!

She snatched it up, causing the coil of chain to slide and begin to snake toward the edge of the chest. She caught it and pressed it to the chest so it didn't fall, but the metal clanked when she did so. She, Kral, and Donial froze in place. After a moment, hearing no response to the sound, she allowed herself to breathe again.

"My mirror," she said happily.

"Yes," Kral said. He tossed her a quick smile. "That is one of the things we seek. Have you any idea where the crown might be?"

"In Koronaka, he kept it in his own room," Donial answered. "So it should be here, I would expect."

But a more intense search revealed nothing. After a few minutes, Kral sighed in frustration. "It is not here."

"Somewhere else in the house, then," Alanya said.

"But time grows short," Kral reminded her. "Those bodies at the gate—once they are discovered, an alarm will surely be raised."

"Father's office, then," Alanya guessed. "We should try there."

"Lead the way," Kral said.

Alanya took the front again. Out of her father's room, with a glance down the empty corridor, then quietly back down the stairs. Every minute they were in the house she was more frightened. What would happen if they were discovered? Would Uncle Lupinius have them arrested? Killed? By leaving them behind in Koronaka and by stealing from them, he had already demonstrated that he wanted no part of his brother's offspring.

But when she opened the door to the anteroom outside Father's office, the dull fear she felt grew to outright terror.

"Rufio," Donial breathed behind her.

He was right. She recognized the Ranger, even though his face was contorted in death.

But worse still was what she saw at the doorway of the inner office.

Lupinius, facedown on the floor. Trailing behind him, a long streak of blood showed how far he had dragged himself.

"Is he . . . ?" She couldn't bring herself to say it.

Kral shoved past her, went to her uncle's side, and knelt there. He touched two fingers to the side of Lupinius's neck. "He lives."

As if spurred by the human contact, Lupinius let out a weak moan.

Alanya rushed to him. "He needs help," she said desperately. "A physician!"

Kral took the man's chin in his fingers and tilted his head up slightly. Alanya saw her uncle's eyes flutter open. "Where is my people's crown?" Kral demanded.

Lupinius blinked again. His lips twitched, and blood showed at the corners of his mouth. Alanya put a hand on Kral's arm. Her uncle was near death, and she did not want him injured any more. "Go easy," she whispered.

Kral met her gaze, then looked away. In his hard eyes she saw unspoken questions. Why should she be concerned for her uncle now? Hadn't he deserted her? Hadn't he most likely killed her father? Hadn't he stolen her most precious possession? She understood these things, and knew that Kral would as soon snap his neck as offer him aid.

Part of her felt the same way. Most of her, she thought. But something held her back. He was still her uncle.

Family.

Blood.

She had cared for him, once. When she was little, before he moved to the Westermarck. He had not come around often, but from time to time he did. He had been funny then, laughing and teasing her. Her parents seemed to enjoy his company, and so had she.

Even after Father had taken her and Donial to Koronaka, Lupinius had not been all bad. Until he had found out about Kral, he had at least made an attempt to be nice to her. It was after that, once he became consumed with the idea of attacking the Bear Clan, that he seemed to lose any memory of his blood ties to her and Donial.

She hated him now, especially for his role in her father's death. Looking at him brought back the full fury she felt when she remembered his corpse, slung over the back of a horse, or lifted reverently onto a flaming pyre. But rage battled in her heart with sorrow.

Hating him was not enough to want him dead.

"Kral," she said, "he needs help."

"We call for help and we'll be calling his Rangers down on us," Kral reminded her. He still hadn't released Lupinius's chin.

"Perhaps," she admitted. "Still . . ."

"The crown," Kral said again, shaking Lupinius's head. Her uncle groaned.

"Gone . . ." Lupinius said weakly. "Stolen . . ."

"By who?" Kral demanded. "Who took it?"

"Kral, do not hurt him," Alanya pleaded.

"He's already dead," Kral answered. "Near enough."

Donial had stood to one side, watching the scene with liquid eyes. Now she turned to him. "Donial, call for aid," she said.

Kral turned sharply back to her. But as he did, she saw his brutal façade melt. "Yes," he agreed, with some obvious reluctance. "Call. Your uncle yet lives."

Alanya was filled with the desire—not for the first time—to pull Kral into her arms. He had every reason to want Lupinius dead, even more than she did. But he had put those desires aside, for her. She longed for the chance to do something as wonderful for him.

Donial moved to the door of the anteroom, stepping past Rufio's still form, and threw the outer door open

wide. "Aid!" he shouted into the night. "Lupinius is injured!"

Kral winced at the sound of her brother's cry. "We
should go," he said. "Now, before they come. There is
nothing more that we can do for him, and staying would be
suicide."

"But—" Alanya began.

"Think you for a second that I will not be blamed?"
Kral asked. "If so, you delude yourself."

Outside, voices cried out in response to Donial's call.
Alanya could hear footsteps rushing across the flagstones.
They would have to leave now. Even so they would likely
be seen. She clutched the mirror tightly, wishing it held answers for her.

"But he can tell them that—" she started. She stopped
when her uncle's body shuddered. Blood flowed freely
from his mouth and nose. He uttered a ghastly rattle, then
was still.

"He will tell them nothing," Kral said. "He is dead,
Alanya."

Her eyes filled with tears for the man she hated. The last
member of her family, save Donial. Her father's father's
last surviving son.

The tears were bitter, stinging. And yet they ran from
her eyes, down cheeks flushed with emotion.

Kral had been willing to try to save her uncle's life. But
they had come too late. Too late for the crown, too late to
save Lupinius.

"Come," Kral said. "Quickly, while we can."

Now Alanya agreed. "Yes," she said. "Run. Run from
here."

Even as she said it, she knew that she would be back.

Her uncle was dead, but in some way, that was almost a
relief. Getting the mirror back was a victory she would sa-
vor. And now there was nothing to stand in the way of getting her house back, as well. The city guardsmen would

support them, and if necessary they could—with Cheveray's help—go to the courts. All the way to King Conan, if need be. She and Donial might be alone, but that didn't mean they couldn't be a family and living in their family home. Here they could rebuild their lives in familiar surroundings.

Alanya felt as if a weight had been lifted from her shoulders. All of her thoughts and feelings had been tentative, somehow, as if she had been waiting for *something* to happen. Now, holding the mirror, standing in her father's house—her house—she believed that it had.

The long nightmare was over. Her father was still dead—would always be dead, just as her mother was. But that didn't mean life came to an end. Clutching the precious mirror, she didn't even care about its supposed magical properties.

She had all the magic she needed, right here. Hope. Optimism. A renewed sense that in spite of all that had transpired, the future would be a happy one. That once again, this house would be filled with laughter and joy and the simple, lasting pleasures of family and friends.

She looked at her little brother, and he was studying her, uncertain. "We're home, aren't we?" he asked.

"Yes, Donial," Alanya said. "Yes, I believe that we are."

EPILOGUE

IT WASN'T UNTIL they tried to leave the house that they were spotted.

Men raced about the courtyard. Someone had seen the bodies at the front gate. Moments after they left her father's office, where Lupinius had finally died, Alanya heard shouts from there as well. Rufio's corpse, and Lupinius's, had been discovered.

They were headed for the back gate, Alanya still gripping the mirror, wishing she could stay in the house. To try to do so tonight would be too complicated, she understood. Kral was right—to be seen here would raise the suspicion that she, Donial, and Kral were involved in their uncle's murder.

Before they reached the stable, however, Donial sneezed. It was a quiet sneeze, and uncontrollable, but definitely audible. A shout from around the corner of the house told them that others had heard it, too.

"Quick!" Kral urged. The three of them broke into sprints, heading for the back gate, and safety. Donial, as usual, was the fastest when it came to running all out. Kral trailed him, and Alanya brought up the rear, though not by much.

She heard sounds of pursuit: the slap of sandaled feet on the flagstones, the clink of metal, the creak of leather. She kept her strides long and loose, trying to put as much distance between herself and them as she could. Outside the gate, she heard Kral shout a command. "Split up!" he called. "We can meet again later!"

She didn't want to do it—he didn't know the city that well, after all. And she felt responsible for her little brother.

But she had promised to obey Kral's orders. And Donial was speedy. He was probably halfway to Cheveray's by now. She couldn't even see him anymore in the dark streets.

So with a last glance toward Kral, she let him go left at the next corner, while she went right. A man sitting inside a doorway alcove called something out to her as she ran past, but she was moving too fast and didn't hear, or care.

Cheveray's house. That's where she would find shelter. That was where she, Donial, and Kral would meet up again. That's where they would take the steps that would restore her family's home to her.

She would take a roundabout route, in case she was still being pursued. But after a few minutes, she hadn't heard anyone chasing her, and she began to relax. Even to smile, thinking about tomorrow, and all the tomorrows after, that she would spend in her house.

All, in some strange way, thanks to a young barbarian named Kral.

She owed him, she knew. She owed him a lot.

She would repay him any way she could.

WITHIN A COUPLE of blocks, Kral was hopelessly lost.

He could find his way through any forest, up any mountain and back down again. But the city streets followed no natural plan. Sometimes they were laid out in square blocks, but then other streets curved. Some ended abruptly, even though those around them continued on for miles. He had run blindly. At last he found himself at a dead end, looking up at three blank walls. He could climb them, he supposed. But would it make any more sense on the rooftops?

Then he heard a voice, and even that option was cut off. "There he is!"

He looked, and saw three of Lupinius's Rangers—sobered by the night's events, he guessed—bearing down on him with swords drawn. There were only three, so he might be able to take them. But they were too close. If he tried to climb, they'd have the advantage. They could stab at his legs, cut him, while he had no way to defend. They'd bring him down and finish him.

Instead, Kral ran straight toward them, his knife in his left hand and the unfamiliar sword in his right. He slashed madly as he neared them, and all three fell into defensive positions, parrying his wild blows. One of them bumped into another with an explosive curse. Kral felt his sword tip scrape armor, and then he was past them, running again.

At the corner, his foot hit a wet patch on the road and almost went out from under him. He caught himself against a wall, though it meant losing his knife, and kept his balance.

But as he rounded the corner, he ran headlong into an armored chest. Barely balanced as he was, he rebounded off it and flew sprawling into the street. Looking up, he saw that he had run smack into the cuirass of an Aquilonian soldier. Behind this soldier were half a dozen others, all in full armor, carrying halberds and swords. Back from patrol, maybe, or guard duty at the city gates.

He didn't know, and really, it didn't matter. He was on the ground, with seven Aquilonian soldiers staring at him in amazement.

And on the other side, closing in again, the three Rangers.

"He's a Pict!" one of the soldiers uttered.

"He's our Pict," one of the Rangers countered. "He's our prisoner."

"Fine with me," the soldier said. "The city guard may have something to say about that, but we'll see."

"I am no man's prisoner," Kral managed to say.

He hoped it was true. But they had him surrounded and outnumbered.

The best Kral could do was hope for a miracle. And the Pictish gods didn't generally provide those.

At least Alanya had escaped. She was the one who had brought this all about. The beauty in the forest, the golden-haired girl he hadn't been able to keep away from. She had her mirror and she would have her home, her brother, her friends. She had a life here in the city, even if he didn't.

No matter what happened to him, he thought, that was something to celebrate.

Looking at the soldiers and the Rangers ranked around him, Kral started to laugh.

Loren L. Coleman

AGE OF CONAN: BLOOD OF WOLVES

In the bleak northlands, Grimnir, the living god of the plundering Vanir, is leading his hordes across Cimmeria. Tales of Grimnir's fury spread as refugees scatter throughout the land to escape his wrath.

In the village of Gaud, the young warrior Kern, the "Wolf-Eye," has been exiled, an outcast from clan and kin. It is he who is fated to confront the dreaded Grimnir.
But as loyal friends and desperate fighters rally to his side, even Kern does not know whether he leads his people to deliverance, or certain death.

0-441-01292-2

Available wherever books are sold or at penguin.com

THE ULTIMATE IN SCIENCE FICTION AND FANTASY!

From magical tales of distant worlds to stories of technological advances beyond the grasp of man, Penguin has everything you need to stretch your imagination to its limits. Sign up for a monthly in-box delivery of one of three newsletters at

penguin.com

ACE

Get the latest information on favorites like William Gibson, T.A. Barron, Brian Jacques, Ursula Le Guin, Sharon Shinn, and Charlaine Harris, as well as updates on the best new authors.

ROC

Escape with Harry Turtledove, Anne Bishop, S.M. Stirling, Simon Green, Chris Bunch, and many others—plus news on the latest and hottest in science fiction and fantasy.

DAW

Mercedes Lackey, Kristen Britain, Tanya Huff, Tad Williams, C.J. Cherryh, and many more— DAW has something to satisfy the cravings of any science fiction and fantasy lover. Also visit dawbooks.com.

Sign up, and have the best of science fiction and fantasy at your fingertips!